THE
SHORT STORIES
OF
RON IDDON

THE
MURRAY RIVER
COLLECTION

Published by Leopardwood Productions, P. O. Box 4818, Toowoomba, Queensland 4350, Australia.

www.leopardwoodproductions.com.au

Iddon, Ron 1940—

The Short Stories of Ron Iddon----The Murray River Collection

ISBN 978-0-646-56272-8

Contemporary life along Australia's Murray River

Book design by Steven Wilson of Cedar Centre, Toowoomba, Queensland, Australia

Virtual Author's Assistant Lyn Prowse-Bishop, Executive Stress Support, Warwick, Queensland, Australia

Type-set in Trajan Pro and Palatino, 9 - 22 pt

Printed and bound by Lulu.com

THE STORIES

A SHORT NOTE TO THE READER

Welcome.

This book is subtitled "The Murray River Collection" because all the stories in it are centred on that river – a waterway that keeps drawing me back to its banks.

You can read these stories in any order – none depend for its sense on your having first read any other. However, since I know that some of us like to read even a collection of random stories from the front cover of a book to the back, I have made some attempt in their placement to vary the subjects and pace – even where possible the style.

Quite a few of the stories are written in the first person, and I have adopted a different persona each time. I hope you do not find this too confusing.

***

These are old-fashioned stories in that each one has a beginning, a middle and an end – though not of course necessarily in that order. I have also tried to ensure that each one *has* a story, in which something actually happens. "The Morning News", which is very slight in story – and in which almost nothing happens – won a national literary competition (!?)

Enjoy.

Ron Iddon
August 2011

ACKNOWLEDGEMENTS

The tremendous contribution by my editor Letitia Gregory of Melbourne; without her many insightful comments, and detailed, constructive suggestions this book would have been so much less.

***

Those friends, and members of my family, who agreed to "road test" many of my early and half-baked efforts: particular thanks to Stephen and Joy Harris of Tamworth, New South Wales, and Bill and Noni Durack of Toowoomba, Queensland. Sadly, Bill is no longer with us; it would have given me so much pleasure to present him with a copy of this book.

***

My friends the black swans who posed so obligingly
– a honk of gratitude.

ONE

BIRDS OF A FEATHER

Vietnam I guessed, as I watched him walk along one of my magazine aisles. About the right age – sixty – and a certain look. I had met quite a few of the veterans over the years.

He was wearing jeans and a black t-shirt under an old loose fitting leather bomber jacket. I couldn't see his footware but I was sure it wouldn't be polished leather shoes. He certainly wasn't wearing the town "uniform" of our local farmers.

It was just after lunchtime and he was the only customer in my newsagency so I had time to observe him. I had not seen this hombre before so I thought perhaps he was just passing through; I guessed that there could be a motorbike outside, though I hadn't heard one pull up.

He wasn't in any sort of hurry, sauntering between my magazine racks. An amazing variety of these today – any subject you like to think of. Occasionally he would stop and take something out, then put it back and stroll on. Big guy – strong looking –

outdoorsey. He'd be looking for something on guns I guessed – or fishing.

He made his selection, came back to me, and put a copy of " Watercolouring For Beginners" on the counter, dropping a ten dollar note on top of it. There you go – my wife is always telling me I jump to conclusions – but then *there's* a case of the pot calling the kettle black.

As I handed the stranger the change I asked him where he was heading. I received an amused look – a "why do people always ask that" look. He held it for several seconds – I thought he might not answer!

"I'm staying here."

"Oh?", and before I could stop myself, "where?"

He held his next look too, as if deciding whether to tell me. I almost said something like "sorry, I'm a nosy bastard", when he said "do you know Col Tanner?" and then, before I could answer, went on "yeah, you'd know everyone here I guess." Said almost *sadly*, as if that were one of the problems of the world, someone knowing everyone. As if it were one of *his* problems.

"Oh, have you taken one of those cabins he has out there?"

"Yeah."

Col Tanner is a member of one of the old families in the district, his farm about ten kilometres upstream from our town. The river does a big loop there and has created a couple of long sandy beaches. Col's old family home is about a kilometre back from the river on a sandy rise – I guess his predecessors weren't taking any chances with being flooded out – but our river is more or less tamed now, with the big dams, and about ten years ago Col built a couple of cabins right on the beaches, to hire out to fishermen and holidaymakers. I'd been inside one of them and it was very well kitted out – very comfortable. I had suggested to Jessica that we might retire to one; she rather thought – Noosa.

"They're very nice. Good luck to you. Doing some fishing?"

"A bit. I'm really..." Again that look, and then he put out his hand. "I'm Brian."

"Kevin." We shook; I gave him his change and he moved to the entrance. There he turned.

"Will you save "The Weekend Australian" for me? I'll be in during the week."

I'll look forward to that, I thought – an interesting newcomer – though possibly not one who needs or wants much company. And yes, I was pretty sure now – Vietnam.

***

When he next came to the shop it was at a busy time. He looked at the magazines again but did not buy any and collected his "Australian". He asked me if I would keep the once-a-month mid-week issue which carried its 'Literary Review'. Prompted by that I told him I'd be receiving Tim Winton's latest during the week and that I had several orders for it already. Was he interested?

He said no, he couldn't carry books around with him, he would wait to see if the local library got it. I suggested he put his name on the reserve list at the library because the book would be very popular.

"Good idea" he said, and was on his way.

***

When Brian next dropped in he asked me if I liked fishing.

"Yes. I've got a little outboard . Go out in it when I can."

"Yellow Belly are biting up at my place."

"You're lucky." Was this an invitation to visit?

"Why don't you take a run up? You might score a beer."

"I will. I'll come today when I've closed up." It was summer and there would be plenty of daylight.

***

He had heard the motor and was waiting on the beach. "See that inlet?", pointing upstream and over towards the opposite bank, "I got my couple in there."

I took his advice and did catch three nice Yellow Belly over the next hour and a half. As I brought my boat back in to his beach again he came down and helped me pull it up. "Not bad. I'll gut them for you."

He did this on a stump in front of the porch – it looked as if it might have been put there by Col just for the purpose. He wrapped my fish in some newspaper and went inside to put them in his fridge.

I turned to look out over the river just in time to see a black swan glide to the water's edge. As Brian re-emerged from the cabin the big bird walked up towards us, not stopping until he was almost within touching distance.

"Amazing isn't it. It's like he's watching me. I call him Hawkeye." The bird flapped his wings as if acknowledging the introduction and then began accepting the small pieces of moistened bread Brian had brought out with him.

When the bird had satisfied himself that there was no more to eat he turned to face the water, gave a honking call, ran forward a few steps with wings outstretched and took to the air.

We washed up in a tin dish at the water tank at one side of the dwelling and Brian went inside and brought out two beers. We settled into two deck chairs on the porch, looking out over the water. The river was peaceful, with no wind to ruffle its surface. The late afternoon sun was turning the water and even the trees to gold. Just beautiful.

***

He did go to Vietnam. He was conscripted in the ballot at twenty. His time there, as he told it, was a mixture of camp boredom, a few tense patrols, one genuinely frightening engagement with the Viet Cong, and some interesting and by and large enjoyable encounters with the local people. "My first sex too. A commercial arrangement but – I wasn't complaining."

Like all his fellow troopers he had been impatient to return home at the end of his service. But when he did he found he had come back to a changed country, the population having turned away from involvement in the war. Instead of receiving the grateful thanks of his fellow citizens he and the other men were met with criticism and hostility. During a Brisbane street march his company was heckled and jeered.

It's a familiar tale isn't it. They had risked their lives and were now being disowned;

I think the effects are with us today. One of my farmer friends here is a Vietnam veteran. He is a friendly man – very community minded – but I see a *distancing* in him, as if he sometimes seems to go to some private place in his mind. He has told me that the antagonism from fellow Australians bewildered and hurt him. His experiences in the war certainly changed him, but so did the homecoming.

Occasionally we get motor bike clubs up from Melbourne to camp for a weekend and one of these is a Vietnam group. "Wild" looking men, with beards, long hair, tattoos and bandanas – they seem to come from a different world.

11

Perhaps there *are* contented nine to five office workers and even successful businessmen amongst them but, jumping to conclusions again, I doubt it. I have noticed that nearly all of them smoke, and I think they drink pretty heavily; I don't know whether I should feel sorry for them, but I do.

***

Brian said that after his return he had not wanted to stay in his home town, where he was well known. He moved up the Queensland coast to a bigger town and took up carpentering, eventually becoming a builder. He married and had three children.

He went into the designing and making of furniture, and it was soon in demand. He charged quite a lot for each piece he said, because it took so long to make, but he found people were prepared to pay. In time he gave away the building business, to concentrate on his tables and chests and dressers, working on his own in his backyard shed.

***

After twenty-five years, and with their offspring gone their separate ways, he and his wife decided to do the same. She was spending more and more time with her women friends and he too found he was gradually withdrawing from their once close union.

It was a parting without recriminations or bitterness, he said, on either side. He described his own feeling as being like relinquishing a heavy load.

Some interest from other women followed, and he did take up with one or two for a while, but he found he was not interested in anything permanent. His wife by contrast fairly quickly remarried, and to her own sister's ex husband.

***

He decided to take off and travel around Australia. At Mataranka in the Northern Territory he looked after a small motel while its owner recovered from an illness. At Geraldton in W.A. he worked on a cray boat for a season.

He said that at the moment he was actually quite busy. He was rebuilding Col Tanner's kitchen, in lieu of paying rent, and a similar job had been promised from a neighbour. And he had taken up watercolours.

**

As I puttered back downriver I reflected on Brian's story. It had made my own life story seem *ordinary* by comparison. I would not have wished for some of his experiences – the war time ones, and that rejection when he returned – and the marriage break-up – but somehow his life seemed more *interesting* than mine.

I had stepped straight into my father's newsagency from school, married the first girl I had gone out with – we also had had three children – but I had always been *here*. I knew everyone and everyone knew me. Jess and I had taken trips, to Cairns and Alice Springs – and New Zealand – but we always came back *here*.

Nothing wrong with that really – it's a good place to live, as good as any and possibly better than most – no crime, no gangs, a strong community feel – but this guy could go *anywhere* – was able to do *anything* – and was seemingly happy like that. A real rolling stone.

I will admit that for a while during that journey back in my boat – just a little while – I felt some envy.

**

Brian would come into town on average twice a week. I asked him to bring in one of his finished paintings. "I might like to buy it."

He shook his head. "They are not good enough. And you might not like it anyhow."

13

"Bring me one *you* are happy with, and that you think I would like."

"No." Firmly, but with a smile. "I'll show you some when you come out again."

Col Tanner told me that Brian was doing a first class job on the kitchen.

***

While I was outside on the footpath one day I watched our visitor walking along the pavement on the other side. There was seemingly an *intent* in his movement, a *purpose*; I noticed that people, even though they greeted him, tended to move a little out of his way. He smiled at them though, and returned their greetings.

The guy has an energy I thought, or *a store of energy*. Some men of sixty here are *old* – almost done with life if you like – but of this man one could believe that on any day he might do something new and unexpected.

***

He asked me if I'd like to come up again – he said he was getting Murray Cod. I said I'd like to come on Saturday afternoon – I shut at twelve – and he surprised me by suggesting I bring my wife. "Drive up; use my dinghy. We'll have a barbecue."

Jessica, who grew up along the river here, loves fishing, so she needed no persuading. We reached his place by two and Jess took a quick look around and said she'd like to try from a fallen tree that we had passed about three hundred metres downriver. Brian said he'd go with her. I took his dinghy and rowed in the other direction.

I went up about a kilometre before I found a spot that looked promising to me. On the way I passed the second of Col Tanner's cabins. I saw nobody there but noticed some washing on a clothesline at the back.

In an hour and a half I caught only one fish, a Murray Cod, but it was a beauty, perhaps five kilograms. As I was rowing back past the cabin I saw a woman sitting on the little jetty there. She waved and I pulled in towards her. As I drew near I realised that she was actually fishing too, with a handline, and I veered away again but she waved me in.

"I'm not doing any good anyhow. Wrong spot probably. How did you go?"

I held up my trophy proudly and she whistled. We introduced ourselves; Ruth said she was on her own. She said she was from Melbourne, and that she'd "had to get away"; I wondered from what.

The woman was fiftyish, medium height, dressed in a shirt and shorts. Bare foot. She had shortish curly hair, black with a little grey. No make-up. She looked fit and relaxed. She looked, I thought, *independent*. Like my friend in the other cabin.

I told her my wife and I were guests of Brian and asked if she had met him.

"Yes – met only." She paused, as if wondering whether to say more. "He seems to be a man that is happy with his own company."

"I think you're right – but he's really quite friendly."

She laughed. "That's good. But I'm – happy to have some time to myself too."

As I was getting back into the dinghy I noticed a black swan gliding in to the beach. My first thought was that it was Hawkeye but then I could see that it was smaller.

"I'll have to feed Princess now. Nice to meet you", and she hurried back up to her cabin.

***

"What do you make of Brian?" I asked Jessica on the drive home.

"Different. Bit of an edge. I don't think he'll be making a splash in our social scene. But I like him. Don't know that he thinks much of us women though."

"Oh come on darling."

"Well – what I mean is – I think he has decided he can get along without us."

"Look, I told you – his marriage broke up..."

"Ten years ago."

"So – he's cautious."

"Mmm... What about this Ruth? You seem to be taken with her."

"I am," playing along. "I think I'll come fishing up here again soon."

We drove on in what they call a companionable silence, Jess's hand resting on my knee. When we reached home she said "it's been a nice afternoon."

***

Jess sometimes helps out in the shop when a lot of new stuff comes in from my suppliers. She was there when Ruth herself came in and I introduced them. They talked a bit and then, a little to my surprise, Jess invited her to our "office" in the back, a curtained off corner of overflowing papers and general confusion. They had coffee, talking there for a long while.

After Ruth had gone Jess asked "did you know she is a nurse?" As Jess had been. "She's coming to lunch on Saturday."

***

We sat at the table on our terrace that Saturday after lunch for hours. Ruth told us she had worked at a big hospital in Melbourne for ten years but had resigned recently. "I found I seemed to have too much to do – I was not able to finish anything to my satisfaction. It's a common thing in hospitals. We never have enough staff. I didn't mind so much when I was younger but it does get to you." She stopped, but I could see it was just to give herself time to choose her next words. "I was 'senior' so I was expected to show leadership and take responsibility, which was alright – but I wasn't getting paid any more. I felt "used' a bit – I am a willing horse but I think I got a little sour.

I had a lot of leave owing but I took the money and resigned. That's what I'm doing up here. Chilling out."

While I did a few things in the garden she and Jessica sat and talked on – quiet serious talk it looked like – and that evening in the kitchen my wife told me the rest of the story. Ruth had been married for twenty years – no children – couldn't have – and she and her husband had eventually drifted apart. She told Jess that although the divorce process had begun amicably enough, her husband had become more and more bitter and angry during it, to the extent that he took to threatening her – physically.

"It got to where she had to get a court order, to keep him away. It must have been awful."

"Is she free now?"

"Yes, but Kev, she said she had been really worried he might ignore the order and come after her. Do her harm. That's the other reason she came here. No-one in Melbourne knows where she is."

"Brian would look after her" I said, without thinking.

"Yes but, you know, she wouldn't want that."

"No. Independent. Like Brian."

"He takes that too far, that independence thing. *You* – you ask me things – ask me to *do* things – I feel I'm important to you. Sometimes."

"Always darling. But you think he's not like that?"

"No. I can imagine his wife – she must have felt unimportant. There's so much of this 'lone wolf' thing about him."

"Well I think he *could* have vulnerabilities."

"But he would hide them. We women like to *see* them. Like – well, *you* – you tell me when you're up against it. You're not shy of letting me see that."

"Well I'm one of those people. Brian would probably think I'm weak or something. But honey, he is a good bloke."

"Men always say that sort of thing!"

"Well he is." I took a breath. "The trouble is you women want to change a man – shape him into the perfect accessory to your life. *Own* him."

"Good heavens." She stood still, looking out our kitchen window.

"What?"

"Do I? I didn't think..."

"No darling *you* don't" – and should have left it at that – "but I have done some work there."

"Oh?", and she turned and faced me, with what I have come to learn is a dangerous smile on her face. "Have you *educated* me?"

I had blundered in, and there was no turning back."Well, putting it that way, yes..."

"And you don't think I have possibly educated *you*?"

"Well – I suppose..."

"You have no idea," and she opened a cupboard door. "Tomatoes on toast?"

"What?"

"For tea?"

***

Not long after that Brian and Ruth came into the newsagency *together*. I must have registered something on my face because Ruth laughed and said "we're saving fuel."

A week afterwards Jess said she saw the pair walking through our river park.

'I saw them too. Don't go reading too much into it."

"I'm not – I think. But they *are* birds of a feather."

***

Next time they came into the shop it was obvious a relationship had begun. And about a fortnight later when they were in again Brian told me that he was about to head back to Queensland. It was time he said to get back to basics.

"Going on your own?"

He grinned. "I'll have company." Ruth leaned around from behind him and also gave a big grin.

She asked me to bring Jess up on the weekend for a farewell meal. We did go, and had a really nice time. Brian invited us to take any paintings that appealed and we chose two. 'Mine' showed the cabin, with Hawkeye standing in front, wings outstretched.

***

A fortnight after they left I went back up the river in my boat as far as their cabins. I did want to try for another Cod but also I was just drawn to the spot.

The cabins were still empty, not yet re-let, and as empty dwellings sometimes do they projected a melancholy air. I continued on to the inlet on the other side of the river where I had caught my big fish, anchored and threw in my line.

***

I was not alone for long. They arrived silently. They were so graceful: magnificent. I fed them pieces of a sandwich.

They stayed with me for fully twenty minutes, gliding around me. Then there was a subtle change in their outlines – a tensing – and their bodies rose and they opened their wings to beat the air. They began to run, their feet just touching the water's surface, faster and faster until they were airborne. They flew upstream, gaining height, and then banked to the left, went out over the trees and disappeared from my sight.

I went on with my fishing but perhaps a minute later I heard again the beating of those mighty wings. They were coming back, fast and low, just above the water's surface in the middle of the river, and straight towards me.

A few metres from me they banked to the right, calling as they passed. They rose above the trees on the opposite bank but this time continued to climb, and I watched them until they were mere dots in the northern sky.

"Goodbye" I said, for I felt that I had just been farewelled.

***

That evening I was watering in the back garden when Jess called out that dinner was ready. Yes, I thought, as I rolled up the hose, and we will have it in the lounge room, because the ABC news will be on – side by side in our recliner chairs, with the little trays on our laps.

And I will look across at my oldest friend at some point and say "this is good Jess" and she will smile and give a little shoulder shake of self deprecation, but be pleased. And we will settle to another easy and comfortable evening in each other's company. Birds of a feather.

TWO

THE MORNING NEWS

I hear them coming along the path beside the river and go out onto the cabin's porch to greet them. Daniel, aged seven, is in front of Ben, who is four. Or four and a half, as he corrected me recently.

They are carrying bowls of Weetbix and milk, holding them at chest height and trying hard not to spill. Both boys are barefooted, wearing tee shirts and shorts. It is very warm already.

Daniel says "good morning Grandpa" without looking up. Ben does look up at me and says good morning too but some milk spills. He says "ooh" and stops to stabilize his load before coming on. The cicadas choose this moment to begin singing.

I sit on the top step of the porch, in the middle, and the boys sit where they always do, Daniel to my right, at the end of the bottom step, and Ben on the other end of the same step. We all face forward, looking at the water, forming a perfect isosceles triangle; where will Basil sit today? He sidles past to my right and goes one step down, to sit between me and Daniel.

I have thought before that it is as if these morning tableaux were being marshalled by some unseen family portrait photographer.

Both boys settle to the task of eating, but I look forward to their news. After perhaps two minutes I see that the four and a half year old has stopped chewing and is staring ahead. He turns his face up to me.

"I heerd a crow."

"Heard" says Daniel.

"I did. When I was in bed." He takes another spoonful. "Crows are bad."

Daniel, without looking up from his bowl, nods gravely and then says "don't speak with your mouth full, Ben."

I say nothing; there will be more on crows.

"They peck sheep's eyes out" says Daniel.

Young Ben swivels around to see how I react to this horror. I shake my head sadly; this is indeed an abomination. Ben continues to stare at me until he believes he has seen the limits of my reaction then turns back to his food.

"Do you know that crows are considered to be the smartest of all birds?"

Now both boys look at me and I tell them that farmers say that a crow can tell if it's a rifle pointing at him or just a stick. "And I knew a woman who had a pet crow, and one day..."

"*A pet crow...?*" Daniel is incredulous. Ben looks from me to Daniel and back again; *could* such a thing exist?

"Yes. She mended its broken leg when it was young and it just stayed around her farm. It was always in the yard. Anyhow, one day she came back in her car and went into the house and left her car keys on a table just outside the back door. When she came out just a few minutes later they were gone."

"The crow took them!" says Daniel.

"That's what *she* thought, so you know what she did?" I am looking at Ben and he shakes his head vigorously.

"She gets her spare set of keys and shakes them in front of the crow and says 'where have you put my keys? I want them back' – and you'd never guess but the crow flew away down the river to a big gum tree. She watched him, and he landed in a fork in the tree and then flew back – with her keys!"

Daniel and Ben do not take their eyes off me. Ben's mouth is open.

"And then he flew back to the tree and returned with a plastic clothes peg. And he kept on flying backwards and forwards for a whole hour bringing something each time."

"What things?"

"Tap handles – golf balls – coins – all sorts of things…"

Daniel resumes eating, thoughtfully. Ben is too full of this to eat – he stares at the bush across the river, keeping very still. Something will come.

"He could have diamonds!"

"Diamonds," mutters Daniel.

"Or – or – spanners" says Ben, perhaps on safer ground.

Hunger re-asserts itself; I sip my tea. Just below me Basil makes a slight noise and does a little kneading action with his front feet which means he wants some attention. I let my right hand move out and down, to rest on his neck; I gently scratch it.

Ben turns towards me; I think perhaps it is to be something more on crows, but his eyes shoot from my face to my hand on Basil and back to my face.

"Do you *like* cats Grandpa?"

"I like cats that like *me*."

"Basil doesn't like me."

Ah, but you are so rough with him. I continue to stroke Basil; Ben returns to his Weetbix.

The cicadas seem even louder. After a few seconds Daniel says "I saw a rhinoceros."

"At the zoo?"

"Yes, and some – " there is a long pause, " – African Hunting Dogs." I am impressed.

Ben is staring ahead, then turns. "I saw a tiger."

We both look at Ben and he realizes he must give us more. His eyes take on an unfocused look, and then, when he is ready, they come alive again.

"Its tail was very long..." and he puts his bowl down on the step beside him and spreads his arms out to their fullest.

"And his tail was hanging through the fence" adds Daniel.

"Yes, and some boys wanted to pull it but it was too far away."

"You wouldn't pull his tail would you?"

"No!", and his eyes widen at the thought. "It would *kill* you."

I wonder how long it will be before Basil 'kills' *him*.

The cicadas stop suddenly, as they do, and the hush is palpable. It seems to be hotter.

Both boys finish off their Weetbix and put their bowls on the ground. Daniel stretches his legs out and I notice how brown they are. Ben folds his arms and leans forward onto his knees. He seems to have found something interesting on the ground. A companionable silence falls over us.

"Ben fell down some steps."

"Where?"

"In a shop."

Ben stares at his legs. Then he stands and climbs up to me, steadies himself with a hand on my shoulder and lifts a knee. On it is a tiny red mark. I give it serious consideration.

"Did it hurt?"

"He cried."

Ben looks quickly across at his brother and I think he is about to deny this accusation but he lets it stand; perhaps it confirms the scale of the incident. He goes back to his place, now limping noticeably.

Another silence falls, and this one continues for some time; Basil becomes bored with it and goes down to sit beside Ben. The boy looks up at me and I lift my arm and make a little scratching movement with my hand and he puts his own hand on the cat's neck and copies me. I hear Basil purring. Ben looks up at me again and I receive one of his best smiles.

I say "tigers are cats."

His eyes widen. "Are they?"

"Yes. The biggest cats there are."

Ben looks across at Daniel but this is obviously old news to him.

We hear a call from my daughter – "Bo-o-oys" – and the two get to their feet and pick up their bowls.

"See you later Grandpa" says Daniel, and strides off up the path.

"See you Grandpa" says Ben and follows. Basil decides that he too is on the move and trails after Ben.

After a few metres the boy turns. "Hurry up Basil" – but Basil hurries for no-one.

THREE

THE APPLE TREE

A licia was there too when he pulled up; she seemed to be doing her mother's washing. He thought of driving on; she should be finished by lunch time.

He hesitated, but then turned into the driveway. This was really the only spare time he had, most of the town's plumbing having decided to fail simultaneously. There would be the usual brusque remarks from her but he would wear them – as he always did. But why was she like this with him? He would have to have it out with her sooner of later; it couldn't go on.

***

He had played the field, and people in the district thought of him as a bit of a Casanova, he knew that, but what they did not know was that for the past two years he had had eyes and heart for only this one. It wasn't just her looks, though he did think she was beautiful – black hair, deep blue eyes – tall and strong, but in a graceful way. No, it was all the other things – how she *was* – how she was *with people* – funny and generous and kind. With everyone except him.

They had known each other for years, from the time he became engaged to her older sister Louise. When that had broken down Alicia had been still a teenager, in her last year of school.

It was odd perhaps but the friendship he had formed with their mother had continued. Monica had Multiple Sclerosis and the illness was developing so fast that she had to depend on friends and family to do things for her. He had started mowing her lawn back then, and had kept on doing it. Now this was really the only place where he and her younger daughter met. But "met" was all it was – they never conversed.

His feeling for Alicia was stronger than he had experienced for any other girls. And different – more subtle and balanced – it was not just a physical longing. Maybe at twenty-six, he had thought, he was growing up. .

But she continued to ignore him. Worse, she seemed to actively dislike him – to have no respect for him. She was abrupt when they met – dismissive – sarcastic even; he was at a total loss to understand why. The best that he could manage was that she resented his break-up with her sister but – for Pete's sake – that had been six years ago! Surely she understood that these things happen.

***

"Good morning Alicia.

"Good morning."

"Big wash this morning?" Brilliant.

"Sheets." She continued walking to the line – no more words.

He pulled the mower out of the shed; it was a big lawn, and with the old Victa it usually took two hours to do. At least he and Monica had decided they would no longer worry about the grass in the little orchard that ran down behind the house to the river bank; then it had taken all morning. He set to work.

He noticed Alicia take two more loads to the line and then she stayed inside – helping Mon there with something no doubt. It was a big pity about the old woman. And he had to stop thinking of her as 'old' – she was probably no more than fifty – but the illness was really taking a toll.

It was a crime that the husband had taken off, and apparently just about the time it had been diagnosed. He had never met the man. Monica had never said anything about him but Louise certainly had, even blaming the man himself for their mother's illness.

When he was on the final section of lawn he saw Alicia come out with another trolley of washing. He made a decision; he would speak today – and, if he found the nerve, tell her how he felt about her.

He took the mower to the shed and pretended to fiddle with it. He rehearsed some lines – "Why don't you like me Alicia?" – "Can we talk Alicia?" – "Can we talk about why we don't get along Alicia?" He waited; she would have to walk right past him to reach the back door.

He stood up and turned towards her as she approached.

"Why do you hate me?"

Not what he'd intended but it was out now. She stopped and stared at him, and he forced himself to meet her direct blue-eyed gaze. Amazingly she smiled – a smile such as he had never received from her before – and it brought a tentative smile to his own lips too.

"Hate you? Yes – I suppose I do." The words hit him like a punch to the heart.

"Why?"

She didn't answer straight away. She seemed to be looking through him, or into the past. He could never have guessed at what was to come.

"I *saw* you."

"Where – when...?"

"In the orchard."

If the first words had been like a punch these were a knockout. And he didn't need to hear any more. He knew she was referring to the time he had made love to a girl – a friend of Alicia's older sister – one afternoon in the orchard. He'd believed they were hidden from view.

He said nothing – couldn't speak. The girl went on. "You did it under the big apple tree. *I was up in the tree.* You didn't see me." Her eyes blazed again. "I could see the whole thing. I looked away, but I could still hear. Everything!"

He dropped his head.

"I was seventeen! And you were going to marry my sister! I was going to be a bridesmaid. And you were doing – that!"

She swept past him into the house, to re-emerge a moment later with more washing. She hurried to the line and began pegging. He went to her.

"Look, Alicia, that was a long time ago – and I am so sorry..."

"Don't apologise to me, apologise to my sister!"

"I did – many times – not for that but other things. We'd had big arguments – we were reconsidering things... and that girl..." His words sounded weak to his own ears; a thought occurred to him. "Did you ever tell her?"

"No. Now go away!" She had tears in her eyes and she waved her arms at him. "Just go away!"

His mind was in turmoil for the next few days. He still went out on jobs but he felt as if he were on auto-pilot. Gradually though one realisation took hold – that that one experience had affected Alicia deeply.

He knew she did not socialise much, and although he would hear from time that she had a new boyfriend, these "friends' never seemed to last very long. Had his act, coming after the desertion by her father, coloured her view of *all* males? Turned her against them? Or was it just against him?

What should he do? *Could* he do anything? If they met somewhere now, what could they possibly have to say to each other now? Could they even bear to meet?

***

He came out of his own house and was walking towards his van when he found her standing beside it.

"These last few days..." she said.

"I know..."

"I'm not sure why I'm here. Can you say anything brilliant?"

"Well – I've got 'I was only twenty'. And 'Louise and I had been having a lot of arguments', but..."

"Yeah." She smiled. "And I've got – nothing," and she punched the side of the vehicle.

"Hey, I've just had the dings taken out of that door!"

She laughed – her first laugh ever with him.

***

They stood, two metres apart, silent, for several seconds. Poised.

"I'm going out to Billy Driscoll's. Fix a leak. Want to come?"

She walked around to the passenger side and got in.

FOUR

THE DREAM TIME

Although it is many years since I captained our country's Test Cricket team my name still surfaces occasionally – when a newspaper does an article comparing cricketers of different eras say, or runs a poll within its readership.

I never make it into "Ten Best Batsmen", though I *was* pretty good, good enough to open. I could bowl well too, medium pace spin, but my forte was fielding. If they do "Best All-Rounders" I sometimes get a mention.

After I retired, at thirty three, I was persuaded by a sports agent to sign up with him for speaking engagements. He thought I could earn some useful income that way and so it has turned out. Even now, thirty years later, I still speak once a month somewhere – Rotary, sports nights, seminars, that sort of thing, and all over Australia – Cairns, Alice Springs, Perth – just last week Broken Hill.

I don't give a serious talk – 'the science of cricket', or anything like that – I mainly tell anecdotes. I do give a short prepared speech – generic stuff about travelling and playing with a team, but then I answer questions. That's the lengthy part, the questions becoming more and more personal about the men in my teams, and my answers becoming more and more libellous. It's good fun.

One thing that always comes up is the question as to who is or was the best cricketer I ever knew.

***

I met Billy Fowler when we were both thirteen, students at a private boarding school at Albury. It was during our first year of Secondary, but well into the year – perhaps August.

The headmaster himself came into our class and told us that a new boy was coming and that he hoped we would make him welcome, and help him to fit in. That man would have known that friendships and alliances had already been well formed by that time of the year, and that a newcomer could have a lonely time of it.

When Billy turned up he was placed at an empty desk next to mine and the master asked me to make sure he had all his correct books and knew where we were up to in each subject; it was quite normal at that school to ask one boy to show someone new the ropes.

***

Billy was skinny, like most of us at that age, but a little shorter than average, and *brown skinned*. His features themselves were not *strongly* Aboriginal; if you took away the colour he could almost pass as white. *Almost* – there was still something about the shape of his face and his body that said 'of Aboriginal descent'.

He was a quiet one, not saying anything unless you spoke first, but because I was a bit of a chatterbox I got as much out of him as anyone. I learned that his home was out in the far west of New South Wales, north of Mildura. He lived on the sheep station where his father had been employed as a stockman; his father had recently left the family, and no-one knew where he had gone. His mother had stayed on, helping at the homestead; Billy had four brothers and one sister, all younger.

His primary schooling had been at a one teacher bush school, a half hour drive from the homestead. He used to be taken there by the station owner's wife, with some of his siblings and her own two children, then the minister at a church in Mildura had arranged for my school to accept him.

***

He talked about his home a lot, and because we were in the same dormitory I would often see him writing letters to his family. By contrast I hardly ever wrote a letter to my family but then I didn't feel all that separated; my home was 'just up the road', on a big sheep stud in the Riverina, where my father was the manager.

I was mad about cricket, even at that age. Back at home I was already part of the district team, playing with the adults, and earlier in this year I had been made captain of the school's Under 13's. We were now just beginning to practice again for the coming season.

One day in, I think, October – I know the days were starting to warm up – Billy asked me to show him how to play. He had never played it but he thought he might like it. He said he was already practising with some of the boys at lunch time, down near the trees at the far end of our oval.

The next day I went down to see what was going on. I was pretty sure they would not be using a school bat because that gear was kept locked away. Even I could not borrow a bat at lunch time.

I was right – they were using just a stick, about the length of a bat but *only a third as thick*, and *round*. 'Stumps' was an old River Red – if the ball hit any part of its trunk you were out.

They were using a tennis ball and most of the boys were *throwing* it, not bowling. There were about ten of them playing and none of the "batsmen" lasted long. They either missed the ball completely

37

or skied it for a catch. There seemed to be some sort of roster for the batting – it didn't just go to the bowler or fielder who got someone out. There were lots of mis-hits; a thin round stick would have been a challenge for Bradman.

Billy was fielding when I arrived. When it came his turn to bat he adopted a stance that no cricketer ever takes – it was more like that of a baseballer, with the stick held almost at head height. He actually stood full face on to the bowler, not side on as cricketers do.

Tony McQuirk, a big boy in our year, and a good bowler in my team, sent the ball down. The ball looked right on target; it was going to hit the tree or Billy's legs – either way, I thought he would be out.

Billy didn't move – not his feet nor his body nor his arms – but at the last moment he swung – and sent the ball back over McQuirk's head. The next ball was a full toss, right at his body; once again Billy didn't move a muscle, not even stepping to one side to protect himself. He faced the ball as before but this time, at the last moment, slapped it down into the ground.

I stayed until the bell rang. In that quarter of an hour not one ball got past Billy, unless it was so wide it was impossible to reach it, and each time he executed this very late swing. He never looked like giving a catch to anyone, yet I knew that off that round "bat" the ball could have flown anywhere.

I learned in class that afternoon from one of the boys who had been playing that Billy had only ever mis-hit a few balls, and that was on his first day with them. Since then they had made him go in last, otherwise no-one else got a turn at batting.

***

I took Billy down to the nets with me that afternoon. I gave one of our good bowlers a tennis ball and asked him to send a few down but only at moderate speed, and coming right onto the bat. Billy told me that he had *never held a cricket bat* and I showed him how *I* held it and how he needed to stand side on to the bowler. I asked for some deliveries and showed him how I made my strokes. I then went down out of the net and walked back up the outside of it to stand near him.

The first ball he missed completely, still on his backlift when it went past – I think the weight of the bat compared to that round stick slowed him – but he made an adjustment to his swing for the second ball. He showed increasing confidence with each ball, beginning to move his arms with something of the speed I had observed under that tree – still with a very late backswing though.

We changed to a cricket ball. The first time he hit this harder ball I could see it jarred him, but once again he was quick to adapt. The bowler was doing a good job, putting all the balls down at a good hittable length, so I moved to the adjacent net to do some practice of my own. Soon though I could tell by the sounds coming from next door that Billy was striking the balls hard. Tony McQuirk took over the bowling, and sent them down faster, but Billy still got onto every ball.

I went to Tony and asked him to pitch some balls further up, making them bounce closer to the new chum. I suggested he drop his pace to start with but I don't think he did – fast bowlers know only one way!

I walked to my position outside the net again to watch. Billy was not ready for the change in length and didn't handle the first ball but he shortened his backswing for the next and got it. He grinned over at me. I noticed he was shifting the weight on his feet now, sometimes moving forward and sometimes back, just like experienced batsmen do. He began to strike even harder, so that McQuirk had to be watchful of the returns.

Billy was right handed, which meant that his left shoulder was pointed at the bowler. Tony decided to start sending a few down that were not at the wicket but that would pass Billy on his left side – his 'leg' or 'on' side. It didn't take Billy long to realise that he could manage these by swinging the bat horizontally and *sweeping* the ball. He hit these hard too, so that, in an actual game, if they had not been stopped by a fielder, they would have reached the boundary.

***

My mind was racing. If Billy could do this on his *first day* ... he could play in my team straightaway – the next weekend!

***

To finish up the practice, and just for fun, I asked Tony to send down a Yorker – that ball that lands right at a batsman's feet and generally right on the wicket – a very hard ball for anyone to do anything with. I went to Billy and warned him. The grin again.

What he did with it made me and the bowler laugh. He planted the bottom of the bat in the ball's path and did a star jump as the ball hit. Appropriate – because I thought we *had* a star.

***

I went to the coaching master and told him what I had just witnessed. He came to practice the next day and straight away put Billy into my team, to bat at number four. There were only three days before the weekend, when we were to play a good team at a town down the river, so we agreed we needed to practice with him every day.

It was incredible how quickly Billy learned. By the Saturday he had mastered not only his drives but those sweeps on anything coming down the on side.

Any ball that was coming straight on but which was at an awkward length he simply blocked; none were going to take *his* wicket. I advised him to leave alone any balls coming down the *off* side and too far out to worry the wicket; there was not sufficient time before this first game to teach him the tricks he needed to handle those.

He also did not yet know how to get runs from a *spinning* delivery but he was able to recognize the little devils when they were coming, and to crunch down on them at the last second. And all his actions were so *quick*.

***

On that first Saturday I was an opening batsman as usual but I lost my fellow opener and then the number three in quick time. The other side's two main bowlers were very good – only medium pace but very accurate – and if I was surviving it was partly luck. I had to content myself with merely blocking the ball far too often, which meant I wasn't making many runs.

When Billy came in, as number four, I warned him about the bowlers. I told him to settle before trying to get any runs. I said he should let any difficult ones – any that weren't right on the wicket – go straight through to the keeper. "Just don't get out" I was saying – I could see us all being dismissed for a miserably low score. Billy and I were really the only chance of our side surviving.

Either Billy didn't understand me or he chose to ignore me. The *very first ball* – and it was a good one, good line and length, – he hit over the bowler's head for four. It was very nearly a six!

And that's how he continued. I suppose there *was* some luck in his innings – he was sweeping at balls that, if he had mis-hit them, could have had him caught – but we piled on the runs. I say *we* but in fairness it was he who did the damage. I acted as the steadier; sometimes he would want to take off for a run when I felt that we would be risking a run-out, and I'd send him back.

In fact though we did not need to do all that much running – very few of his balls did not reach the boundary. I thought at first he was just having good luck in getting them past the fielders, but after a while I realised that he was *placing* them. The other captain was ordering a lot of field changes to stop the flow of runs, as I would have been doing in his position, but Billy then hit the ball into the newly created gaps.

***

I was the captain, and up to now had been by far the best batsman in our team, but this day I played second fiddle. I went only after the safe balls, basically concentrating on not getting out. This was something I would do many times in my later first class career when my partner was "hot", but this was with a partner playing his *first game.*

At the end of my side's batting innings both of us were still at the crease. I had a respectable score – something like fifty – but Billy had over a hundred.

***

For the next week Billy was the talk of the school. The sports master was euphoric."We will win the comp!" I heard him tell other teachers.

I said that we needed to do much more practice with Billy. The master wondered if we *should* – might we be interfering with his natural ability? I told him that there were things we could easily improve without cramping his natural talent – and Billy still had to learn what to do with balls coming down the *off* – not to mention the spinners.

I was a classical bat already at the age of thirteen – people commented on my stroke playing and general style. I had been lucky enough to go to a special fortnight's coaching school in Melbourne the previous summer, just before I had come to the school, run by two great ex-Test batsmen, and my weaknesses had been ironed out. Not that I had that many I suppose, but there is always something to learn – and I had been more than ready.

I thought it would be great if we could get Billy to one of these schools, but in the meantime I could pass on to him as much as I had absorbed from that school.

I taught him how to roll his wrist, so as to pass the face of the bat over the ball and thus prevent it from rising for fielders to catch. Also, he was still very loose and mobile with his head and upper body carriage when he was preparing to hit a ball; I showed him how the correct position, and stillness, could help him make a surer shot.

I was able to show him what *I* did with that off ball, the one coming down his right side, just touching it with a turned blade so that I used the speed of the delivery itself to send it away. In the years ahead I would make countless runs, even score lots of boundaries, from those nicks.

As for the spinning ball, I could tell that he was already able to *see* the spin, and to set himself for it.

And all the time he watched me with total concentration – it was almost unnerving. He would copy me – and very quickly get it right. To my chagrin. What had sometimes taken me months to learn he seemed to master in a single afternoon!

***

Seeing the ball – that is something no-one can teach. Really gifted batsmen see the ball as it leaves the bowler's hand, as if they have magnifying vision, and as if the ball is coming in slow motion. I never had that – not *exactly* that. If I got 'set' early for a delivery it was more because I could read the bowler's intention, from his run-up and the action of his arm and the lean of his body. Even, sometimes – it's true – by the expression on his face.

Billy Fowler though seemed to have the eye of a hawk, which they say is able to see the tiniest movement on the ground, even from a great height. Sometimes, if I were standing near him when he was about to face a delivery, I would hear him give a little grunt as the ball left the bowler's hand; his computer had processed it.

The other thing that I would not have been able to teach him – would not have even tried – was *dash*. I was not a dashing batsman – correct and careful, and just occasionally bold – but not dashing. Billy was *all* dash, and with his wonderful eye he only needed to learn technique and he would have it all.

***

Each afternoon we had him down in the nets. One day the sports master brought in bowlers from our senior team, the Under 18's. A couple of these were big hunks that could send down rockets. The master had instructed them not to bowl bouncers, or anything directly at Billy's body, but as I watched I still felt some trepidation.

Their first ball was low and really fast, but well away from the stumps. Billy let it go.

I was standing at my usual mid off position just outside the net. After the ball went past Billy stared at the spot where it had hit, frowned, and looked back at the bowler.

He didn't touch the next ball either, which was just as fast but this time much closer to the wicket. He walked forward and tapped the pitch where the ball had touched. That done he looked over at me and gave the grin that I was becoming accustomed to. Whatever else it meant, it said 'watch this'.

The next ball came down just as fast, Billy rocked back, executed a very short backlift, and hit it straight back at the bowler. Classic. From then on he was onto every delivery.

It was wonderful to watch. My pint sized friend put away every ball that the biggest and fastest bowlers in the school sent down.

***

Johnson, the sports master, called me into a conference with Mr.Wilmot the headmaster.

I had seen the two together the day before, during practice, standing some distance off. They had been joined by two other men I did not know. All four had stayed for quite a while.

Wilmot now told me that the men I had seen were cricketing administrators from Melbourne and that he had asked them to come up specifically to watch Bill. He told me that they said he was the best for his age they had ever seen and that he had to be booked into their next school in Melbourne in January, the same one I had attended the previous summer. In the meantime they would ask someone who happened to live locally to come along to the school and give him some coaching.

The man they mentioned was a legend of the game, a man second only to Bradman in stature and reputation. I had never seen him bat – he had retired in the 1920's – and I had never even seen any film of him in action, but this was like being told we were about to be visited by one of the gods!

The man – I'll call him Clarrie B. – had knocked up some huge scores during his career. One of my older uncles had seen him in action at the M.C.G. and always reckoned that he beat the Poms that day all by himself.

He would by now have been in his seventies and actually lived nearby in Wodonga, our twin town just on the other side of the river. The reason for this conference was to get my view as to how Billy would respond to this man.

"Who wouldn't?" I said.

"Yes" Wilmot said, "I think we know *you* would, but – well – Billy's getting a lot of attention lately. The local paper wants to do a story – take some photos. It'll probably get on the front page. I think you know Erskine?" I did – their sports writer; he had even done a story on me. Second *last* page...

"You know Fowler better than anyone here, Mr. Johnson tells me. Is it affecting him do you think?"

I was flattered. Being asked for my opinion – by the *headmaster*.

"I think he'll be alright sir. He's very, very keen. He loves all this."

The men looked at each other and nodded and that was that.

***

'Clarrie B.' came over the next afternoon – he seemed *very* old to me – and now we began the most intensive sessions.

Clarrie – he did not want us to call him mister – still had 'the eye'. We borrowed one of the Under 18 bowlers, one who had a reputation for accuracy, and Clarrie told him where to place the ball. Then he began to make adjustments to Billy's technique.

I stayed close by – my own bat in hand – watching and listening for all my might. Clarrie gave Billy a rest now and then and I took the opportunity to practice what he had been imparting. He knew of my role in all this, and he included me as much as he could.

He was inspirational. And so polite and friendly, and humble too; he would have been a great 'role model' as they say for today's 'celebrity' sportsmen.

On our school sports afternoon each Wednesday we set up full matches and Clarrie volunteered to act as umpire. He gave advice to all and sundry; our whole school was being coached by the very best!

I think he got really caught up in it all, so much so that he would come with us on our weekend fixtures – where we were now beginning to trounce the opposition by bigger and bigger margins. But Billy remained Clarrie's focus.

***

One day in late November Billy was called from class .When he returned he sat silent and serious. After class he told me that his mother was very sick. She was in the Mildura hostpital and she wanted him to come and see her.

The headmaster sent for me the next day. He said that he had arranged for Billy to go to Mildura on the next day's bus; we had a service then which travelled right along the Murray valley. He said the mother had a serious liver condition and she might not come out of hospital. It was possible she knew this, and that this might be her last opportunity to see her son.

Mr. Wilmot was talking to me as if I were Billy's brother but that didn't seem at all strange; we *were* like brothers. He said he was very worried about what might happen in Mildura. How would Billy cope, seeing his mother in such a bad way? And when he met all his brothers and sisters again? The local minister had arranged for temporary homes amongst members of his congregation and for the children. He said that the trip could be a very difficult one for Billy.

Straight up I offered to go with Billy. Mr.Wilmot thanked me and said he would clear that with my parents; I learned later that he had already talked with them the night before. He must have had a good idea that I would make the offer.

***

It was a long trip in the bus; we left just after daybreak and did not arrive in Mildura until after dark. The minister took us straight to the hospital. I waited outside when Billy went into her room, but after a little while he came out and said his mother wanted me to come in too.

She was so much more Aboriginal in appearance than her son that I got a shock. And she was obviously very ill, thin, with sunken eyes. Weakly she thanked me for coming with Billy. She seemed very tired, and in just a few minutes, while the minister was talking, she fell asleep. We stole away.

We went down to the hospital twice the next day. The first time the woman was sleeping so soundly that even when Billy shook her – gently – she did not wake. The mind sometimes takes indelible photos doesn't it, at certain moments, and that was one. I can still see Billy bending over his sleeping mother, his light brown hand on her much darker shoulder.

The second time we called she was awake and very alert. She wanted to talk about their times back on the station. Billy joined in with his recollections. The mother and the boy laughed a lot about things that had happened; I got the impression that life there had not been too bad.

She talked to him about his brothers and sister, but this became so personal, and I could see that both were so affected, that I made some excuse about going to the toilet and went for a walk. When I came back after a quarter of an hour she was asleep again. The minister lent us some rods and we went fishing in the river,

The next day the minister took Billy around to the various homes to see his younger brothers and sister, then we both visited Mrs. Fowler, again twice during the day. She began to include me in the talk with Billy as if I were one of her family – as if I too had lived with them on the station. Sometimes she would be looking directly at me and would say "Do you remember that time...?"

She was animated, her eyes bright. Once she talked about her husband. As she told it he was a good man but restless by nature, finding it hard and eventually impossible to stay in one place. She asked us – asked *both* of us – not to think badly of him for leaving them.

She also said she wanted Billy to go back to the school. We told the minister this and he went down to see her that night to confirm, and booked us on the next morning's bus.

A fortnight after we returned to school Billy's mother died . He did not go back for the funeral – did not want to – and I think I understood. He had seen his mother and they had said their goodbyes. Now, with his mother dead, and his father's whereabouts unknown, and his brothers and sisters living in a variety of houses, Billy was pretty much on his own.

But he – *we* – had our cricket. We continued to smash the other teams in the district – not only could no-one get Billy out but he began amassing huge scores. We started to get crowds at our matches – for the *Under Fourteens*! People asked for Billy's autograph.

***

At the beginning of December the headmaster called me in again. Did I know what Billy was going to do in the coming holidays? With no parent in Mildura and with his brothers and sister somewhat scattered he had no real home to go to. Would I find out what Billy was thinking.

It seemed that Billy wasn't thinking of anything. He was very keen to go to the cricket school in Melbourne in January but other than that he had no plans. I thought – why didn't he come home with me?

It would be terrific to have him at home I thought; I had only two sisters, and both younger. If he were there we could go fishing in our waterhole on the creek in our dinghy, and go shooting rabbits, and I could teach him to ride my pony – a lot of things. I was sure my parents would agree.

Wouldn't you know – I received a letter from my mother saying that if Billy had no place to go during the summer break why didn't I ask him to come home with me? Old Wilmot it seemed had been busy again.

That December was the best time I ever had at home. We did all the things I hoped we would. Dad had a few jobs lined up for me and some of them could have been a bit of a bore, like checking fences and cleaning water troughs and collecting fuel for the wood stove, but these things were enjoyable with Billy along. It *was* like having a brother, and the better because we were of the same age.

Before Christmas Mum took all the kids to our town beforehand so that we could buy presents. She had got around the fact that Billy had no money by paying him and me for some of the more onerous chores, like cleaning out the shearers' quarters and chipping burrs. It was a neat answer, and paying me too made it seem fair dinkum; I had never been paid for anything before!

Mum and Dad really took to Billy. Not that they had long conversations with him; you didn't. Dad wasn't much of a talker either, but he and Billy would happily spend the whole morning or afternoon in each other's company, doing some job or other.

"By gee that kid's got a good eye," I remember him saying. "He can spot a flyblown ewe before I can." High praise indeed.

Sometimes I would catch Mum just looking at Billy. One time she turned to see me watching her and she had tears in her eyes; she smiled and winked. That is another of those 'snapshots' that have stayed with me.

And of course there was *the cricket*. The season was well under way by the time we arrived home but our district team was always short of good batsmen and we were rushed into the side. They were particularly keen to see Billy in action – they had heard about him from my parents – and he did not disappoint. Actually he was a sensation. Once again no-one could get him out, and he piled on the runs. Our team had a golden few weeks.

But then – oh, but then – a week before we were to take Billy down to Melbourne there was a phone call from the Mildura minister. The father had been to see him. He wanted Billy to come back, to come out to live with him on the sheep station where he now had a job, about a hundred miles north west of Broken Hill.

There were phone calls from Mum and Dad to the headmaster and to the minister – even to a solicitor friend in our town and a government department. *Could* the father do this – what about the boys schooling, let alone his outstanding promise as a cricketer – what if they offered to *foster* him – eventually, what if they offered to *adopt* him?

But – the boy was a minor and his own father wanted him to come back and that was that.

It was to me the most awful news. I would be losing my best friend – my "brother" – and the school and, who knew, the *country* would be losing a wonderful cricketer – the most promising cricketer *anyone I knew* had ever seen! What chance would he have to play out west of Broken Hill?

My mother pursued the schooling angle – surely his education would suffer – but the minister said that the station was a very large one with a lot of staff and as it happened the wife of the manager had been a secondary schoolteacher and would see to Billy's education. My mother argued that his present school would be able to do much more for him; I overheard her offering to pay his school fees, and asking the minister to tell the father that. Dad offered the father a job on our place. To no avail.

***

We took Billy down to a town on the Murray and put him on the bus – and our home became a sorrowful place.

We received a short letter from Billy two weeks later, just before I was due to go back to school. He was on the new place and he said it wasn't too bad. The manager's wife he said was a nice lady, and he was also earning some money in his spare time doing jobs for the owner. There was no-one to play cricket with though.

I wrote back after I got to school, telling him about our new teachers and the new sportsmaster. I told him how my cricket team was shaping up, and again begged him get his father to change his mind.

For weeks afterwards I would stop whatever I was doing at school if a bus pulled up at the gates, to see if a skinny brown kid might get out. How I wished that would happen.

I did not receive a reply to my letter and though I sent another I did not get a reply to that either – and now I know why.

***

The Broken Hill turnout that I addressed last weekend was huge and the questions kept coming for what seemed like hours. I told my story as usual about Billy and afterwards a woman who was the wife of one of the organizers introduced herself; she said she was Billy's sister.

I looked quickly around – was he here? As she watched me do this her hand came out slowly towards me. On some instinct I also reached out and we grasped each other's arms.

"Billy died. You didn't know? He got killed just after he went to that place."

I was as shocked as if I were still that boy of thirteen. I slumped into a chair and Sally sat beside me.

"How?"

"He fell off a windmill. He went up to get rid of a bird's nest. He broke his neck."

I can tell you I was as grief stricken as if it had just happened.

When I had collected myself I asked why we hadn't been told at the time. Sally said that *no-one* had been told, not even her and her brothers. There had been a quick inquest in Broken Hill and he had been buried in the town's cemetery. She said that she thought the reason their father had not told anyone was because he felt responsible. "He might have felt shame."

None of them saw their father or even heard from him again; the man they had called Dad just disappeared from their lives.

She said that all of them had done the rest of their schooling in Mildura and that her brothers had spent their working lives on farms. All four were still working and were healthy and she saw them regularly.

***

"William Alan Fowler 10.3.43 – 22.2.56 Gone To God "

The grave site was neat and tended. "I come here sometimes" the woman said. She walked away, to tidy up another person's grave she said, but I think she knew I wanted some time alone with my friend.

I sat on the gravestone and talked to Billy. I mean, I really talked to him – aloud. I told him about making the Australian Eleven and eventually making Captain. I told him about some of the best scores I made, and where I made them. I told him I was usually one of the opening pair.

I told him that when I made the Under 13's early in the first year at that school I had dreamed of someday playing for Australia – of opening the batting. Then when he turned up and we started to play together I had changed my dream to include him.

"Imagine Billy" I said, "us – *the openers!* How good would that have been."

How good would that have been.

FIVE

YOU JUST NEVER KNEW

Emily was thinking she might have had time to go down and let the hens out of their yard when she heard the Landcruiser in the distance. She believed she recognised its sound – though she *was* expecting it.

Her niece probably wouldn't stay for a cuppa but she put the kettle on anyhow. She put out some Anzac biscuits too, though the girl probably wouldn't eat any of those either. Always in a hurry, that one.

"Hullo Aunt" as the girl rushed into the kitchen. "Look, I won't have a cup thanks, I'm in a hurry. Dentist at nine." It was seven thirty, and it took an hour and a half to get down to Albury. Emily handed her the short shopping list.

The girl was halfway up the hall to the front door again when she rushed back. "Oh – news. The boys' dogs killed all of Aimee's ducks."

Emily froze. One of her continuing fears was that the pig dogs would swoop on her own birds one day. Aimee McDonald's two boys and Tanya's younger brother were on a mission to clean out the wild pigs in the hills above the river, and all the farmers were for it, but they didn't keep their dogs under proper control.

"They've gone out again today – up this way. Keep your precious girls locked up."

"Poor Aimee. I'll ring her a bit later." And she *would* keep the birds in their yard, instead of letting them have the run of the garden and orchard as she had intended.

She loved her nephew, and the McDonald boys too – the three were like her own sons, in and out of all three houses since they were little. She hoped they did call in on their way home – they knew there was always a welcome – but this business with the dogs; why didn't they keep them locked up on the back of that ute!?

When her niece drove off and she had put the biscuits away she put on her old straw hat and walked down to the chook yard. As she reached the gate some of the hens came running.

"You think I'm going to let you out, don't you. Well, not this morning." As usual it was Hillary and Therese who reached her first and she bent over them and stroked their backs. Most of the hens allowed her these liberties. They were all like her pets really – she knew each of one of them; there were over fifty, but each one had a name.

She was very glad she had originally decided on the Wyandotte breed – pretty *and* productive; over the years she had culled out the poorer layers, and any off – type or flighty ones, and had bred her replacements from only the best. "Poultry Keeping" had sent someone to write about her, and take photos; they said she now had one of the top flocks in the country. Since the article in the magazine she had had more orders for settings of eggs than she could fill.

Money from the sale of chicks and eggs had come in very handy over the years too, especially when the wool sales had been so low. She reminded her husband of that whenever he grumbled about "all those chooks". Get real dear, she thought, liking that phrase that she sometimes heard the boys use.

***

She collected twenty-three eggs and went back to the gate. Andy's special gate. His special fence too – "The Wall of China" her sister-in-law called it. Well a chook fence had to be secure here, there were so many foxes around at night. Andy had done a marvellous job.

As she closed the gate she noticed that the iron peg that the latch rested on was getting loose – the hole it went through had simply weathered over the years. But the thing she would have to ask Andy to look at was the weight suspended on a cable that always ensured the gate swung shut. It had always worked perfectly, and when the gate did slam shut the latch came down automatically – that was marvellous too. Andy had installed it the day after they had returned from town one time to find the previous gate open and all the birds out in the orchard. But now that cable was catching a bit.

Nothing unusual about the birds being out in the garden and the orchard, but she only let them out when she was home; the odd fox did prowl about in daylight. And the trouble was it wouldn't just kill *one*; they seemed to go mad and kill everything. She had often wondered why that was.

And even when she *was* home she only let them out if Ralph stayed with them; she was quite confident he wouldn't let a fox or strange dog anywhere near the birds. He was always so alert – but for a Blue Heeler, remarkably gentle and forbearing too. She would sometimes see hens pecking at things right between his feet, and even little chickens perching *on his back*.

Andy had taken the dog with him this day over to the Fitzpatricks. He'd said he might be useful with the cattle job they were doing, but she suspected it was mainly for the company. Ralph was good company.

She rang Aimee McDonald and found the woman really wanted to talk about her loss. The worst of it was, she said, she'd been home at the time. She normally shooed her ducks into their pen when she heard the boys' vehicle coming back, but this time she had had the radio on. She'd run out when she'd finally heard the shouting but couldn't do anything – they killed all ten of them. The dogs hadn't taken any notice of her or the boys.

"We'll really have to insist they tie the dogs up in the ute." Emily said. "I suppose they'll call here later. I've decided it keep everything locked up today."

"No, it's alright now. We've put that big old cocky's aviary on the back of the ute – you know the one we had under the tank stand? It's big enough to walk into. There was no proper catch on the door but we wired it up. So our poultry should be safe from now on Em. I'll get some more ducks I suppose."

***

After lunch she went back down and collected another twenty eggs. In the heat of the day most of the hens were staying in the shed; a few were quietly poking about in the shaded areas of their run. The four roosters seemed to have taken time off from their duties too; they were squatting together under the lemon tree – like men at their club, she thought.

There was a pine stump that the roosters hopped onto when they wanted to crow and she sat on that. Some hens walked over to keep her company.

***

She had always liked chooks, from when she was a girl on her family farm down on the plains, and she had been allowed to have her own little flock. She had taken real pride in keeping the household supplied with eggs. She hadn't liked it when her mother or father decided that they needed one or two for the table – they were her *friends* – but she had compensated by hatching out some more chicks.

When, in her thirties, she had announced to her own family that she intended to keep chooks once again no-one had been particularly surprised; they *were* surprised at how much reading she did beforehand, about husbandry, and the different breeds.

She didn't know anyone who had Wyandottes but she very much liked the look of them, from photographs – alert, with solid bodies. Nice *shapes*. They were said to be friendly and docile, and the really good thing was that they came in many colours – gold, silver and buff, as well as black and white, and some with spectacular markings, like the Lace-Wings. The breed laid well too – two hundred eggs in a year was quite normal.

She had ordered two settings, and from two different breeders, to give herself separate bloodlines, for when she would eventually be breeding her own replacements. She'd put the eggs under two of her sister-in-law's broody Rhode Island Reds. She went up to "Gunyah" every day to check on them and after they hatched – twenty two out of twenty four eggs – she took each hen with her brood and settled them in the little hutches Andy had built. She reared all twenty two, and was lucky in getting fourteen pullets.

She identified each with a numbered coloured band on its leg; today some of her hens had quite a collection of "bangles". Not that she really needed that help – she knew each bird by sight.

***

Two years after she bought the first eggs she began to set a few of her own. Andy quizzed her about her long term plans and she told him she would eventually like to keep fifty hens. He said 'lets do it properly then', and put up two big sheds, each big enough to divide in two, if she ever needed; he put up the Wall of China."

The "Wall of China" she had christened it – over two metres high, with the netting buried half a metre into the ground, to stop foxes from digging under. Andy used small gauge netting which was good because it kept little chickens in and goannas out. It had seemed to keep snakes out too; although she had seen snakes in the garden and orchard from time to time, she had never seen one inside the run. It was impregnable.

Later Andy had added the gate with the weight and cable mechanism; it was foolproof.

***

Emily had received a letter one day from a woman asking if she could buy a setting of fertile eggs. She lived a good two hours away down on the plains but said she had heard about the flock; she was prepared to drive over to collect the eggs, and was willing to pay *twenty* dollars. Emily was amazed – but that sale led to two others in quick succession and she realized she had the beginnings of a business. "Emily's Wyandottes" was born.

She sought advice from other breeders about the best and safest way to send eggs, and she researched packaging and postal rates, and train timetables. She put her roosters out with the entire flock, to get more fertile eggs, advertised in "The Land' – and was swamped with inquiries.

Many buyers didn't seem to know much about Wyandottes so she made up a brochure about the breed, with photos, eventually expanding it to include general advice about poultry husbandry.

People who had no hens of their own asked if she would sell day old chicks. As some of her lesser layers went broody she gave each a dozen eggs.

***

These days she received phone calls and letters from everywhere. People asked if they could just drop in, to see the birds and have a chat. She sometimes thought that, now that their girls had left home and there was plenty of room in the house, she should provide accommodation – a sort of 'Poultry B and B". Andy was not keen about that, but she would see...

She had loved it all. Sometimes it had got a bit hectic – and her family had complained that she was not giving them the time they felt entitled too – but then things quietened down again. And the money she made was important to their budget. She doubted if Andy still really understood how much of the household expenses were being met by "Emily's Wyandottes".

***

One of her girls – Millie – was sitting in her lap, something she had always done from when she was a fledgling. She would settle as if on a nest; Emily half expected to find an egg there one day.

She now lifted Millie, placed her on the ground, and walked to the fence. She *could* let them out she thought, now that the boys had the dogs locked in on that ute; she was still tossing that up as she reached the gate when the phone rang .

Andy had set up an extension bell on the outside back wall of the house and it was very loud – she could hear it from the very bottom of the orchard. She had decided that as the day was half over she would leave the birds in. As she hurried to answer the phone she did not pause to close the gate because she never had to – it closed by itself; that was the beauty of Andy's weight and pulley.

Because of the noise of the bell she wouldn't have heard this time the bang of the gate against the post, let alone the click as the latch fell into place – *if those things had happened*. But the fraying cable had caught in the pulley, and the gate remained fully open...

***

Up in the hills the boys had had no luck. They had gone to several promising locations without seeing a pig. At much the same moment as Emily was rushing to the phone they were once more loading the dogs into the cage on the back of the ute. One of the boys twisted the tie to secure the door – and didn't notice the wire come apart.

As the vehicle bounced its way back to the road the wire fell away completely. It would now take only a touch from any of the dogs and the door could swing open.

***

At four o'clock Emily decided she should make a pudding for dinner. She had her noisy old mixer going when Tanya arrived. The first she knew of the girl's arrival was when she walked into the kitchen from the front hall.

"I've parked out the front Aunt – I'm in a hurry."

As you always are my dear. She took the supplies from her and the change, and gave her niece in return a billy of fertile eggs, each carefully wrapped in newspaper; Tanya had said she had a broody bantam.

"Slip them under her tonight."

From the front door the girl called back "Watch those boys and their dogs Aunt."

***

When the boys came they always parked behind the house, near the old tank stand. She thought she just might take a look out the back, to check if all was as it should be, but the timer on the stove sounded and she went instead to stir the sauce she was making for the pudding.

About five she heard a vehicle. This'll be them, she thought, and began to make up a jug of cordial. The vehicle pulled up; she began to break up some ice for the jug; she heard a dog bark.

***

Just before dark, while she and her husband were having dinner, her niece rang.

"You haven't seen the boys Aunt Emily?"

"No. I thought it was them earlier but it was your uncle. Are you worried about them?"

"Oh, not really. Mum asked me to ring. They are a bit late though"

"I'll ring you when they get here."

She didn't tell her niece that it was only when Andy had called out to her that she had found her chooks spread right through the back garden and the orchard. She had hurried out and they had put them in together, and then looked at the cause, the cable jammed in the pulley. Andy said he'd replace it the next day.

***

It was after eight and she and Andy were watching television when Tanya rang again.

"Aunt Emily – the boys won't be calling. They rang us from the Gerrahty's"

"Nothing the matter is there dear?"

"They're pretty upset. All the dogs are dead."

"What!"

"You know that old shepherd's hut near Black Spur?"

"Yes. I haven't been there but – it's deserted isn't it?"

"Yes, no-one's used it for years. But there's a spring there and people have said they've seen pigs."

"But – the dogs – ?"

"You know they've been baiting for dingoes on the Range – 1080 – it's deadly stuff Aunt. It looks as if someone in the plane made a mistake and dropped baits all around the hut. The dogs just – well you know how they are – they ran everywhere and picked up the baits before the boys realized. The gate on that aviary was open. They all died."

***

Making their late night cocoa in the kitchen, she didn't know what to think. She was sorry for the boys – but what if that hadn't happened and they had come here ... with all her birds out and those dogs loose...?

You just never knew sometimes, she thought. In this life you, just never knew.

SIX

LIONS

I have been owner and editor of our local newspaper here in this town for over twenty years and during that time I have known three Catholic priests who gave up their vocation. The first two left the district as well – to do just what I do not know – and I thought it was probably a good thing that they chose to start their new lives somewhere else. I could imagine that it might have been hard for those men to blend into life here, and there could also have been some awkwardness for members of our community too; an ex-priest who had heard their confessions might have known rather too much about their lives.

The third man though, Bill Glanville, has not left, and in fact runs a business here; within a month of being decommissioned he started up a garden nursery.

I had liked Bill, and I resolved to support his new business as much as I could; just a fortnight after he had begun, and when I was ready to plant some more shrubs, I went down to "The Greenery". There were quite a few other customers there too.

"Business looks good Bill."

"Yes. Run off my feet."

It would have taken a lot to run this fit, broad-shouldered individual off his feet. And he did not look his age; I knew he had just turned sixty but he could have passed for forty five. An energetic man with a cheerful, positive nature.

***

He loaded my few shrubs into the back of my utility. They were in large pots, so they were quite heavy, but he handled them as though they weighed nothing.

"That article Daniel did on me for your paper didn't hurt. A lot of people who come in here have told me they have read it."

"Well, thank you for agreeing to do it. But I think you will do well anyhow. Do you feel happy about your big decision?"

"Had to happen, Frank. But, um – I'd like to tell you something."

He lifted the last pot into the vehicle, paused a moment and then leaned on the side of the ute beside me. "Frank – I'm letting all my friends know this – I am gay."

My turn for a pause. "Is that why you left the priesthood?"

"Pretty much. It was a secret I was tired of keeping. The church, well – you know its attitude on that. And then there's the celibacy thing; I don't go along with that either."

I thanked him for telling me and wished him all the best. I drove home – but now, instead of thinking about where I was going to plant the shrubs, I thought about Daniel.

***

Less than three months before, in November, a Year 12 boy had come to my office looking for some work experience over the summer holidays. He intended to do a university course in journalism in Melbourne; were there any opportunities for him to do some reporting here in the meantime – any assignments he could work on?

As it happened I was thinking of doing some longer articles – interviews with older residents of our town and district, about their life and times. I had already approached a doctor, a school principal, a storekeeper, a farmer, an ex-dingo and rabbit trapper, a sawmiller, a mailman – and the Catholic priest. All had agreed to take part.

I had already thought I might ask a couple of my friends to do some of the initial interviewing – gathering the basics as it were – and I would then complete the articles myself. Daniel would fit into my plans neatly.

The lad presented very well – polite and well spoken – nice looking too; he reminded me of my son. He gave me the name of his English teacher as a reference and when I rang her later she said the boy was a good writer, and particularly good at research.

In time I ran through with Daniel the names of the potential subjects. He said he already knew Father Bill from some coaching the man had done with his cricket team. I rang Glanville and he said he remembered Daniel. "He should do a good job."

I told the budding journalist the kind of thing I was looking for – a personal story, but with plenty of dates and place names and other references – at least 3000 words.

"Come back to me anytime you want, or if you have any difficulty – if you feel you do not have the man's full co-operation. But I don't think you'll find that."

This lad was just eighteen but I was struck with how confident he seemed. Very much at ease, with me and other adults around the paper. He was *ready*.

***

Daniel rang me two days later to say "I have heaps – and I'm only up to his twenties! I'll have a lot of re-writing and editing to do but I'm looking forward to it. He's leaving the Order you know." I did know this, but not what he was intending to do; I said that I assumed the man would be leaving town and that's when I learned that the man was intending to stay and start the nursery.

***

I bumped into the priest outside the newsagent's and he told me he was enjoying being grilled by Daniel. "I think he's writing a book!" He commented on the confidence of his inquisitor. "He's some dude – *very happy with who he is*" – words I would later reflect on.

"He told me you are quite definite about leaving the Church?"

"Not the Church. Just this" and he touched his collar. "Long story." I wondered if *that* story would be part of the profile.

Daniel phoned at the end of the week to say that he thought he now had all he needed. I asked him to run through his intended approach; he did so and I thought it sounded fine, and told him to go ahead and do a first draft.

***

From some of the things Daniel had told me about the man's early life he certainly had an interesting subject. Glanville had come from a well-to-do grazing family in the Riverina and had gone to a private school in Melbourne, where he had become a top athlete. He had gone to military college and into the Army, had served in several war zones, making lieutenant colonel by the early age of thirty five. He had not married, and had left the Army to train as a priest. A real 'Christian soldier'.

He had been in our town for fifteen years and I have to say had been a real asset. He had coached teams in a variety of sports, and trained boys in athletics. He was a good musician and had a good singing voice; he was first choice for any charity concerts we put on. He had a great interest in gardening, and kept the grounds of the church and the presbytery looking wonderful; he did a monthly column of gardening advice for my paper.

It had surprised me to learn that he was going to stay here, but I thought that if any ex-priest could get away with it *he* could. The nursery idea sounded good.

As for the reason he was leaving the priesthood, Daniel had told me that the man had said merely that he felt it was time to move on. Looking back now I think that they may have been *Daniel's* words, not those of his subject; there was certainly no mention of sexual orientations.

***

Daniel's first draft was very long but read well. Rather than use the red pencil myself I asked him to have a go at editing it down. He did a good job of that, keeping the essentials and removing the parts that could safely go. I thought he displayed good story telling sense.

When he had wrapped it up I gave him a few short news assignments and then turned him loose on two more "old timer" profiles. He did well with those too, and then in late January he went off to Melbourne.

***

Now, in late February, I had called to buy the shrubs, learned about Bill Glanville being gay – and was beginning to think about Daniel's work. I wondered if the priest had told the young man that he was gay, and I guessed that he probably had – interviewees usually tell us journos much more than eventually makes it into the finished article – but if so, Daniel *had not passed that on to me*.

So, apart from displaying journalistic ability, the young man had also shown, at the very beginning of his professional life, a quite remarkable degree of discretion.

Then I began to worry a little. Inside this journalist is a conservative rural man. I began to think – and here I am aware I that I am revealing an attitude that could well do me no credit with many people – that perhaps I had been remiss in placing the youth in a position where he had had to work closely and on his own with a gay man. My mind raced away with possibilities – had Daniel *not* mentioned the priest's sexual inclinations to me because something had happened? Had he perhaps been compromised in some way? Had I, unknowingly, sent this Daniel – to use a biblical reference – into the lion's den?

Daniel seemed to be a well balanced kid, and "normal" – code if you like in *my* way of thinking for "straight". I told myself that he was unlikely to have been influenced by associating for a short while with a gay man. But I did not know the lad well, just as – pretty obviously – I had not known Bill Glanville well.

These were silly thoughts – I shouldn't probably be acknowledging them – but I was unable to dismiss them. In my defence I need to say that I am *not* one of those people that confuse homosexuality with pedophilia – for all I know half of Daniel's teachers might have been gay. But I asked myself, if it had been my own son who had come to me wanting to work on the same project – and he is friendly and open like Daniel – would I have knowingly put him with a gay priest? I had to say I would not.

***

I got Daniel's Melbourne address from his father and posted the whole interview series to him. I also included a note asking him to ring me.

He did and we talked about the uni course – he said he was loving it. I said there had been very good feedback from his article on

Glanville. I told him about the man's business and how successful it seemed to be.

"By the way" I said, trying to sound casual, "he has come out – as gay."

"Oh, okay."

"Did you know he was?"

"Yes." Said matter of fact. No big deal.

***

Later in the year when I was again buying something in Bill Granville's by now bustling nursery I was served by an assistant, a man of about thirty years. I met Bill on my way out and commented on how helpful I had found his assistant.

"Actually he is my partner."

"Oh, are you expanding?"

"No, my *partner*" and he held my eyes and smiled. The younger man was near us, within hearing distance, and I looked across at him and he smiled at me too. The penny dropped.

***

I have just met young Daniel again, three years later; he has just finished his studies. He is visiting his family here and dropped into my office. Bigger – a handsome *man* now – and, if anything, an even more relaxed and confident individual.

He has a friend with him, Toby, who did the same course at uni. Toby was Dux of the year, and both are now on their way to the same big regional city, where they have secured positions on its daily paper – the start to their careers.

They told of pranks they got up to at uni. It was obvious that they are close friends, and that they have spent a lot of time together.

They finished off each other's stories, even individual sentences. In that they were like a couple.

***

At the end of an entertaining hour, as I walked them to our front door, Toby excused himself to go to our toilet and while he was gone Daniel said "you know that time you rang me and told me you had learned Bill Glanville was gay?"

"Yes." I wondered what was coming.

"You were worried about me, weren't you?"

"No. Not at all." I felt some embarrassment.

"Yes you were," grinning, and very sure of his case. "You were worried Bill might have tried to hit on me."

I was red faced by now. "Look, I *was* a bit worried, but..."

"Frank, I was eighteen – I was cool with it."

"Oh well..." I was lost for words and it must have shown. He chuckled and gave me a gentle punch on the arm. He was having fun.

"Would you like to know if he did try?"

"Yes. No! Look..." This lighthearted young man had me completely discombobulated – to use that good old-fashioned word.

Toby emerged and Daniel called "hurry up partner."

Their car was parked right outside. At the car Daniel turned. "Bill didn't need to tell me he was gay."

"How did you know?"

He winked. "My radar."

They drove off, but not before I saw something that gave me a jolt, something that drove the thought of going back into my office from

72

my mind. Through the rear window of the car I saw Daniel give Toby a kiss: not a long kiss, but – definitely – a kiss.

I decided to go for a walk, and headed down the lane that runs beside our building and which leads to the river. I was discombobulated again.

***

Bill Glanville had said that he found Daniel a delightful individual. But I was recalling that he also said that the lad was "very happy with *who he is*." Was this what he was referring to? Had Bill Glanville been interviewed, at the very time that he was contemplating "coming out", by someone who himself had no doubts about his own similar sexual preferences?

If so, then my earlier fancy – that the priest's office might have been some sort of lion's den – was so wrong. Ridiculous. Instead it might well have been more like a haven – a place where two men communicated, and got to know each other, perhaps also lending each other confidence to face their individual lives ahead.

***

It is beautiful on the riverbank here under our big Red Gums, and I decide to take a long leisurely stroll. We don't take as many strolls as we should, it seems to me.

SEVEN

THE THINGS WE DO

"Where's Jenny?"

"Dunno."

"*Don't know*. And go and find her please."

"Aw geez."

"Please Andy. I rely on you to keep an eye on her."

The boy mooched away and just then one of the twins at her feet let out a squeal. She turned the dough out of the big dish onto the floured table top, stepped back carefully and looked down, but whatever it was that had made one of them call out seemed to have been resolved. Both boys were engrossed again in the wooden toys scattered around them.

She turned back to the big table – the only thing about the house that *was* big. House!? A hut really, just four rooms and a narrow verandah. And so hot. The Riverina in January was bound to be hot, she had known that, but couldn't someone have used a bit of imagination? No insulation in the ceiling, no shade trees either, and the heat coming from the low iron roof of the verandah made the house even hotter.

The man who had given Reg the contract to grade the roads and tracks on this station had not been very factual in describing the place. Or perhaps he had been, and Reg himself had done the misleading. That was possible; he had been so keen for her and the children to join him.

"It'll be good-o. You'll have everything you need. It'll be great for Andy and Jenny too – get them used to farm life."

She had been doubtful – it had sounded a bit *too* basic – life would be a lot more comfortable for her and the children if she stayed at home in Melbourne Her mother's home really, but their's too since Reg had returned from the Pacific. But each time now that he had got a job or a contract in the bush he wanted his family to go with him.

She could have played the pregnancy card this time, she would be seven months by the time his contract cut out, but all her pregnancies had been trouble free, and they would be in Echuca on the Murray well before the baby was due. And then their own farm!

Her mother had exploded. "Are you mad! What for? Stay here – there's plenty of room."

"Reg wants us there Mum."

"Well it's selfish of him, that's all I can say. Miles from anywhere. It'll be hot as blazes. There's – there's – snakes, and – and – no *electricity* for heaven's sake – and – you're just about to have a baby. What if its twins again?"

"It's not Mum. And I'm only five months."

"Six!"

"Five and a half." She had hugged the woman – someone who had told her often enough how her own husband, who had come home weak and sick from France, had hated to go anywhere without her – had scarcely let her out of his sight.

"I want to go Mum. You know."

She couldn't – wouldn't – hold it against Reg for their being there. She knew she wouldn't ever really understand what it had been like, those wasted years; this was little enough to give in return.

She and Reg had had only two weeks of married life – just long enough as it happened to conceive Andrew – before he had been sent from Melbourne by train to Townsville and then on to active service. Two years later she had managed to travel to Brisbane when he had had a brief furlough, miraculously conceiving Jenny in that time – but she had not seen him again until late in 1945.

Her mother had sold her little house in Collingwood and bought a larger one at Murrumbeena on the southern fringe of the city, "for all of us" she said – but Reg didn't want a city life. The Government had set up a settlement scheme for returned soldiers and their number came up in the ballot for one of the new irrigated farms on the Murray. While they waited for a house and sheds to be built Reg was taking any job he could get to build up their savings.

***

Andrew walked back in. "I can't find her."

"Stay here – watch the twins. And keep the flies off this." She started for the door but changed her mind and went up the little hallway; the girl might have been been sleeping somewhere inside.

She went quickly through the rooms, even looking under beds and in the wardrobe in her own bedroom. The laundry! – but that little room at the edge of the verandah was empty too. She did a quick circuit of the verandah, calling loudly and scanning the surrounding paddocks as she went – and now a thought that had been on the edge of her mind rushed to the centre. The pond!

A shallow creek that crossed the paddock on the southern side had a little tributary that filled a depression just a hundred yards from the house. This waterhole was only the size of the house itself, and shallow, but Jenny had been forbidden to go there – Andrew too, though he had already been taught to swim, and she was fairly certain he went there anyhow; did he think she never noticed the dried mud on his feet?

"Run over to the water, quick!"

The boy took off, spurred by a tone of voice he had not heard from his mother before. She watched as he disappeared into the thin band of trees surrounding the water and as he reappeared a minute later.

"No!" he called, and kept running towards her. She checked the twins and then sat on the bench just outside the kitchen door; the baby was kicking.

The boy arrived back, panting.

"You'll have to go and get ..." but he interrupted her.

"She's been there."

"How do you – what did you see?"

"Her footprints."

She shot to her feet. "Stay here", and started for the water.

"You'll need me Mum. I'll see better."

That was probably true – the boy had already developed "bush" eyes. She went back inside the house and placed the playpen around the toddlers. As she passed the rising dough she picked up a tea-towel and threw it over it. She shut the door carefully; only last week there had been the snake.

The boy ran ahead of her and took her straight to the footprints on the muddy perimeter of the pond, but even she would have seen them. They followed them around the edge until they turned and *went into the water.*

"Oh Andy!"

"It's alright Mum, it's only shallow. Look." and he walked straight in. When he stood in the centre the water was still only up to his waist. He smiled at her – but a three year old could drown in it. He could see she was not reassured and he said "I know, let's go around the edge and see where she came out." They did this, going in opposite directions, but she was gripped with fear – until the boy called "Mum! Over here."

There, near the little overhead tank that Reg pumped into when he needed to take some water out to the grader, were the sweet little prints coming away from the water.

"Let's look right around the water" she said; the child might have gone back in again.

This time she asked her son to walk with her because his eyes really were so much sharper than hers – but there were no more prints.

On the way back to the house she told the boy she wanted him to go for his father. "You do know where he is?"

"Yes. The white gate."

"You're sure you know the way?"

"Mum." Scornfully. "It's straight along there", pointing to the track that ran due west.

"How far...?" she started to ask, but he didn't yet know distances. Reg had said the white gate was about a mile away.

"Not far. I can run."

"No, don't run." It was so hot – he could get heatstroke. " Just walk. I'll give you a little waterbottle. Where's your hat?" He probably would run, part of the way at least.

Half way back to the house they heard one of the twins crying and she told the boy to run ahead. She thought of the snake. When she got there he was holding Ben.

"I think he's thirsty," he said.

She got a tumbler from the cupboard as Johnny started to cry too. As she gave them both a drink she had a feeling of déjà vu – it was just as she was doing this the week before that Andy had burst in shouting. They had run out and thrown sticks at the nasty creature till it had left the verandah and then the boy had dispatched it with some rocks. It had been a Brown too. It had shaken her up.

Andy was almost out through the door when she stopped him. "No, stay here. I'll go."

"Mum, I'll be quicker!"

"I know but..." The boy was only five; she just couldn't send him out there; what if *he* got lost? "It's – I want you to stay here – look after these two." And as an afterthought, "Jenny could come back in."

"But then *you'd* be here Mum. And anyhow you won't be able to ride..."

But she shushed him and put on her wide straw hat and took his water bottle from him; she had made up her mind. "You are the man of the house now. Keep the boys in the pen."

"What if they cry?"

"Andy, let them cry. Or give them a nurse. You know what to do darling – you're good with them. We won't be long." She hugged him and headed off briskly. At the house gate she looked back; he was standing on the verandah, and already with one of the boys in his arms; he was a wonderful kid. She waved and he waved back; she knew he was itching to change places with her, would put the baby back in the pen in an instant and race to her if she called – probably why he was still watching.

She resumed walking but more slowly now. I have to be sensible, she thought – so many people get into trouble on hot days like this. And I am just a bit burdened. If Mum could see me now. *The things we do!*

She looked back again; oh to see the little girl on that verandah.

After twenty minutes or so she stopped and when she turned was surprised at how far away the house seemed. I'm doing well, she thought – but just then the baby started moving again. She walked across to a nearby Red Gum and stood in its shade while the baby did his exercises, and for fully five minutes.

She realised she had been thinking for some time now that this one was a boy. *Another* boy... but that was alright, as long as he was perfect – like the others.

But where – where – was little Jenny? Could the girl have gone to see her Daddy – come along this same track? She continued walking, looking now for little footprints.

She stopped to take a drink. She found she was still comfortable with the heat, though it must have been a hundred. Well it was *always* a hundred – but somehow this was not as hot as in the house.

After another fifteen minutes of trudging she stopped again – she thought she had heard something. She strained for the sound, and there it was, faintly – a motor – and as she listened it got louder – until around a bend just ahead came the little Ferguson tractor, Reg at the wheel, the little trailer behind – and sitting up the front of the trailer a smiling fair haired girl.

An astonished man brought his tractor to a halt in front of a now broadly beaming woman.

***

He told her that he'd come back to the pond to fill up the drums with water and Jenny had appeared and said that Mummy had said she could go back out with him. As it was only another hour to midday – and he had told his wife that he would be coming back to the house for lunch anyhow – it had seemed reasonable.

"But darling we never let Jenny near that water!" And then "oh never mind now" and she continued to hug and kiss one bemused little girl. Time enough later to talk to a little criminal about disobedience and telling fibs.

Reg lifted his wife up onto the trailer beside his daughter but before he had gone a hundred yards she called for him to stop. It was too rough; "I want a bouncing baby, but not bouncing inside me." She suggested she drive the tractor – he had taught her to do that – but after he had helped her up she found she couldn't fit behind the wheel.

She tried standing beside him while *he* drove but there wasn't room, and in any case the tractor was even more bouncey than the trailer.

***

The boy saw that the dough had risen well; he had never seen it so high. He wondered how high it *could* go. Then he thought he should knock it back as he had seen his mother do. He always thought that was funny – "knock it back" – like it was a cricket ball! But he'd always wanted to do it.

He pounded the dough with his little fists until it was well and truly "back" and then thought he might as well go on with it, and divided the lump into two, shaped them and put them into the loaf tins. He took the tins over to the slow combustion oven and slid them in. He thought it didn't feel very hot.

The twins were both asleep and he thought it should be safe to run over to the woodheap for a couple of extra pieces. He went to the doorway – and stopped in his tracks. Just pulling up at the gate was his father; he hadn't heard him. On the trailer was Jenny, now waving like a mad thing, and back along the track – a long way back – was a figure, trudging slowly.

His face screwed and he rapped one fist against his side. People don't listen! I told her she wouldn't be able to ride back.

EIGHT

TERRIBLE ME

Everyone says it's hard being a single mother and it is; I've been one now for three years.

Right now I'm sitting with another one, my old girlfriend Tanya. She's *always* been a single mother: one boy and one girl. She's never had a partner; someone "donated". *That* I find a bit weird – but it takes all kinds.

Thing is though, Tanya is a bit soft with her two. She lets them walk all over her. Good kids basically but if *I* had them for a month there'd be some changes.

Her latest whinge is that they won't pick up after they've been in the bathroom. Well that's easy to fix and I tell her exactly how. She says, and I know its coming, "you're terrible Muriel", but I get that a lot, since that Toni Collette film, and especially since I *have* apparently become such a witch.

Her kids come in from school. They go straight to the fridge – pretty much like mine do – but Tanya says aren't you going to say hello to your Aunt Muriel and I get the briefest acknowledgement. If I had those two...

***

At the time my Reg took off our eldest Alan was fourteen, Natalie thirteen – now there's a difficult age – Rebecca was eleven and little Reggie was six. We were living, and still do, on a farm about an hour upriver from Wodonga. Reg is in Albury now with his Chantelle or Chartreuse or whatever her name is and yes I know that's a colour but I can't be bothered remembering her name. Anyhow, a hairdresser – twenty three.

I've asked myself what she saw in him but to be fair Reg is not a bad looker – black hair with blue eyes – always a good combination I think. Young Reggie has got that too. But looks only take you so far, eh.

***

When Reg and I hooked up it was at Wodonga High, when I was only fifteen. He was hanging around the school gate one day and just walked home with me. Typically slack of him really. We got hitched when I was twenty and he was twenty-two; I can't actually remember him *proposing* – but that would be Reg too.

He was an only kid, and when we married his parents moved into town and we took over the place: sheep and cattle. The farm wasn't big enough to give us a decent living though; it would have been for his parents but with the costs of everything going up it wasn't any more.

It was a struggle for five or six years but then Reg took up a job selling drenches and cattle blocks and that sort of thing to farmers. He liked the travelling, and being from the land himself he spoke the language, so he did alright.

***

Was it a surprise when he left me? Well, yes – it was a bit *imaginative* for one thing – but not such a surprise on the other hand. He was never all that *connected* to me, if you know what I mean. And as for taking a real interest in the kids' school work and thinking about what they might do with their lives – forget it.

And do I miss him? Well – he *was* useful – if something went wrong with the car or machinery; he was good with those things, like a lot of country blokes. And as far as *that* was concerned well it was never very exciting; put it this way, he wasn't one for a challenge. He would have got one with this Chantal I'd say.

No, really the main worry has been *all the extra things I have to do,* like mowing the lawn – it's a big lawn too – and fixing fences and dripping taps and leaks in the roof. I've had to learn a lot.

The slacker does come back to lend a hand with the big things, like mustering and shearing, but all the rest, like checking water troughs and moving the stock, is left to me and the kids. Alan's pretty good with these things now though, and Natalie is getting handy.

***

What I started to talk about – looking after the kids – that's the hard part. For one thing, there's the time it takes to run around after them – or should that be running *them* around. I have to take them to the bus or in Reggie's case to the school in the village and pick them up afterwards and then take them to sport and anything else that's on. Rebecca does ballet half way to Wodonga and now Reggie practices in a band which is just as far in the other direction. I'm just a taxi driver most of the time.

I had a good think a few months after Reg bolted and I decided I could keep on top of everything if I got co-operation. Do you get that Tan, and all you other mothers who have been told things by your kids about what a monster I am? Just some *co-operation* – and a little bit of effort; those two things, I thought, and I might be able to manage – and who knows, eventually be able to hand over to the world some half decent young adults.

The first thing I tackled was the daily mess in the house. The kids just left things everywhere – like most kids – but it had to stop. One morning after I cleaned and tidied up as usual – I remember it was a Sunday – I decided that *this* would be the day; at teatime I made a speech about how we all needed to do our bit and they could help by putting games and toys away and taking clothing back to rooms. There was the usual lack of response; well, they were *eating*.

When the last of them had gone to bed that night I surveyed the disorder and chaos in the lounge room and the rumpus room; I swear I could not have walked from one side of either room to the other without stepping on or into something. I picked up the plates and cups and glasses and took them to the kitchen but the rest of the stuff – the socks and pullovers and games and toys and tracksuit pants and comics – I dumped all together in what we call the mud room, which is just inside the back door.

The outrage the next morning was something to behold, but I got the impression that a lot of it was because they felt their own precious things had been *contaminated*. It was like what I've heard about in India, where the castes don't touch each other's possessions. They tackled the heap like a school of piranhas, and it disappeared in a minute.

I made something special for breakfast and there was even joking about piranhas. Reggie reckoned *I* was the piranha.

After I returned from running Reggie to school I looked around and it was still a bit of a mess but I tidied it up; gettting kids off to school in the morning has to create some mess. But that night I repeated my warning. Natalie did take her stuff to her room when she went to bed, giving me a dirty look on the way, but there was still a fair heap that went to the mudroom. No outrage the next morning; if I had to describe the mood I would say 'sullen' By the end of the week though – no more problem.

Next project was getting across the difficult concept of returning one's dirty plates and cutlery to the kitchen. I couldn't employ the mudroom solution because there would have been too much confusion, not to mention breakages. Identifying each person's plates and putting them in their rooms wouldn't have worked either – they would have stayed there until they had disappeared under mould.

I got around it by doing a washing up roster, with each night a different one collecting things and helping *me* wash up – or me helping them. It has still meant work for your's truly but it's been good because I get to actually talk to my children, one on one. If I ever wrote a book on this I would include a chapter on doing jobs with your children. Somehow when they are involved in something they open up. It has to be a fair dinkum job though, like ironing or bed making or weeding the garden.

I made sure the kids knew the washing up roster was serious, and any backsliding was met with retribution. For instance, once Alan found he had taken a totally inedible lunch to school with him – *cheese sandwiches*. Imagine!

"Mum how could you forget I *hate* cheese?!"

"I don't know – it must have been be the extra work I have to do, like washing up on my own. It makes me tired and forgetful."

He really has mastered the black look. In fact all of them are quite gifted in that department; Natalie is the best.

The bathroom was next. Just like Tanya's kids mine left their clothes where they dropped them. I told them one evening that any clothes that were left in the bathroom would be assumed to need washing and would be put by me in the dirty laundry basket in the laundry. Once again, complete indifference. Wouldn't you think they'd have learned?

When I went to the bathroom about nine o'clock that night there were four untidy heaps of clothes on the floor. I scooped them up and dumped them as threatened. In the morning there was name calling as before, plus "I can find only one of my socks" and "I had a five dollar note in my pocket and now it's gone!" I was compared very badly to all the other mothers they knew; Alan wondered if what I had done wasn't actually *criminal*.

But that evening though there was only one heap – Reggie's. I contrived to carry it past him in the hall and he grabbed it and took it to his room.

***

The lawn. It must be six times the size of an ordinary town block. Reg had always done the mowing, with our old Victa, sometimes roping Alan in to help. When Reg took off Alan lost all interest and it was more or less left to me, but I could barely manage the time, and Alan and Natalie always had excuses; in summer, with the heat and rain, it needed doing more than once a week.

I drew up a roster – including myself, to make it seem fair – and said I was not going to do anyone else's share. I took the first turn – but then the grass got longer and longer, to the extent that even the kids were saying they were embarrassed by it – but not embarrassed enough to actually do anything about it.

I refused to give in; the grass reached half a metre in places. Rebecca was disgusted – with *me*. "How can you stand it Mum?" Reggie said he did not want any of his young friends to come over any more. "It's gross!"

Finally it wasn't me that cracked or the kids but *Reg*. He turned up one day in December, went away again – all the way to Wodonga as it turned out – and came back with a ride-on. Now I can't get the kids off it.

The pets were next. I think its good for kids to have animals to look after but that's it – *look after*. Every day I was finding I had to do something for them that their owners had overlooked.

Rebecca likes bantams, and since we have a rooster, we often have cute little balls of fluff around the place. We do love them but so do foxes and hawks, and Rebecca was giving those critters just too many opportunities. I used to ask after dinner if they had been put away, and she and I would often have too go out in the dark looking for them.

I told her that if she forgot to lock up her current little family I would take them away. It happened again, and the following day while she was at school, I put them in a box and took them up to the barn, with some feed and water. When Bec came home and looked for her darlings I told her that I had given them away. She got angry and cried a lot and then promised that if she could have them back she would never let it happen again. I told her where they were and she went and brought them back. Abused me of course – and I know there are women who would say I deserved that – but she is good with them now.

I did much the same thing with Reggie's finches. I kept finding that there was no seed in the dish or water in the drinker. I explained – for the tenth time – that little birds cannot live very long at all without feed and water. I said that one day he would find them all dead; I threatened to give them away.

Within a week he let it happen again and I took the cage to Bernie Cargle in the village who has lots of birds and asked him to mind them for a few days. That worked too.

***

My present project is the flyscreen door. It's just off the kitchen and if you don't close it carefully it bangs shut with a tremendous noise. Tremendous to me, but apparently unnoticeable to any of my brood. I have asked all of them, including Visitor Reg, to please close the door quietly behind them, but because it has this big and very effective spring on it they don't see why they should bother.

"The reason it makes so much noise Mum is the bottom half. If it was all wire you'd hardly hear it." And it *used* to be; the masonite that's there now is because their dogs destroyed the wire.

91

One night at dinner recently – that's the time I make my pronouncements – I showed them a clipboard with a sheet of paper and their names on it. I said that each time I heard someone bang the door I was going to put a cross against the name – blue for the first time, black for the second and red for the third.

"What about the fourth time?" Alan smirked. My kids do good smirks.

"There isn't going to be a fourth time" I said mysteriously and, I hoped, worryingly.

I hung the clipboard up beside the door and by the time they had gone off to school in the morning there were several blues and two blacks. This isn't going to take long I thought, I'd better start planning my responses.

The first to reach red was Alan, as I was sure it would be. This was on a Friday afternoon. The next morning when I was trying my hand at dyeing an old pullover of mine his tan "second best " jacket fell down from the shelf above the tubs and into the dye. It came out a mixture of cream and blue. He was ropeable. (He had earlier told me he would like me to dye it black, and I knew I would be able to re-do it.)

The next to get a red cross was Natalie, and that same morning. As it happened she had taken a dress out of her wardrobe and hung it on the line to air; we were all going that night to a dance at the local hall. She pedalled off up the road to visit her best friend – I do have a healthy and energetic mob of kids – and during the late afternoon I absentmindedly turned on the sprinkler in the back lawn. The dress got soaked.

"Didn't notice! How could you *not notice*? You must have walked right under it! Oh Mum, look at it. I'll never get it ready for tonight."

What I *had* noticed earlier was that she had two other nice dresses laid out on her bed so I knew there were alternatives.

The next morning, at breakfast, I ran a pen through those first three entries of both Alan and Natalie. Just afterwards, while I was still in the kitchen, I heard the two whispering at the back door and I thought – this'll be interesting. Natalie came into the kitchen and sat at the table. I could feel her looking at me. She's thinking *"could my mother have watered my dress deliberately. And dyed Alan's jacket?"* I could not meet her eyes, and found it hard to keep a straight face; it's not easy being Terrible.

Reggie went into the red next. It was the day before he was to play some football in the village and when he went to get his ball in the morning he found it was flat. He had to cycle to *his* friend's property to borrow a pump

***

Reg visited and I told him what I was doing and went to get the clipboard and added his name.

"Cut it out!"

"Cut it out nothing. *You* are the biggest problem .Where do you think they all learned it?"

"Yeah, well, I'm never here, so it won't affect me."

We'll see, I thought. He let the door slam on his way out to the shed and I called out "that's one." His two others came up that same morning. After lunch he took the boys to the back of the place to shoot rabbits. When he came back and was ready to drive away he found that unfortunately he had a flat tyre. Reggie had to cycle the two kilometres again; I didn't mean to penalise *him* – but he likes any excuse to ride that bike.

Alan got a blue again, then a black and then a red, all within twenty four hours; I sometimes wonder if he isn't a bit slow. His jeans went into my wash the next day and when he came back from school I saw him run straight to the line and go through the pockets. I was berated for washing something without checking the pockets –

" – there was a ten dollar note there Mum! You've gotta be more careful."

Two days later I gave him the note; it was on the shelf in the laundry. I *am* careful.

***

They were all in the kitchen one afternoon after school, eating bread and jam as usual, when Natalie said "Mum, we don't think you've been acting honourably." *Honourably.* I looked as innocent as I could.

"Come on Mum, you know what we're talking about" added Alan.

"No, you'll have to tell me."

" Well – the back door."

"Oh," I said, and hurried out to get my clipboard. "This is good. Only one – a blue – on you Alan. I want to congratulate you all."

Natalie was looking down and I thought I saw the beginnings of a smile. Then she looked up and she *was* smiling "You're *bloody* terrible Muriel!" Well that was a twist – the mouths of the other three dropped open.

That night I took them into the village to have pizzas at the little café. They're not very good – we do much better ones here at home – but it seemed a good time to do it.

***

Reading this back it strikes me that this would be a good place to end this story. I wonder if I sent it off to one of our rural newspapers they might publish it – with a few name changes of course. 'Tips from a Rural Single Mother' – something like that.

"But wait," as the man in that ad used to say, "there's more" – but not about the kids.

I was having a cup of tea with Reg – in the kitchen – just a few days ago. He'd been fixing Rebecca's bike in the shed, and was now making short work of some cup cakes I'd made. They're his favourites, with sultanas in them. And yes, I did make them especially.

Anyhow I noticed he was edgy – uncertain – as if something not good was happening to him, and I *knew* that he and Chartrelle were splitting up. This didn't make me happy but it did make me feel – something.

We were sitting opposite each other and he was looking anywhere but at me; I said what is it? I didn't really want to hear the details – but I got them anyhow.

He said they'd been having arguments lately and she'd been working very long hours. I asked if he thought she had met someone else and he said yes, he'd seen this guy, a young bloke, parked outside the salon a couple of times.

He looked at me and smiled and said – get this – "the call of youth to youth"; where did he get *that* from?

It's *her* flat and he said he would have to move out and I realized straight away that he was working up to asking *if he could return*. I played dumb – as I can – and asked if he was looking for somewhere to stay in Wodonga and he said not really. I asked what he was going to do and right then he said he was thinking he'd like to come back.

I played even dumber and said that I had heard that the people that worked on the Gilchrist place were leaving and the house they rented in the village would soon be free. He looked sort of helpless at that, God love him.

***

He mooched off to do something in the shed – letting the screen door slam of course – but I know it won't be long before he tries the charm thing on me.

Just as I'm getting this single mother thing licked too.

NINE

NEVER TOO OLD

Up until five years ago my wife and I had a fruit block in an irrigation area on the Murray River. A recurring lower back problem forced me to give up the work and we moved into the local town.

This is a busy place, with some history; there's a big Red Gum sawmill, still working, and a huge old wharf, and paddle steamers that do a nice trade with the tourists.

We've taken to our new lives; my wife is into everything about the place, crafts and charities mostly, and I'm busy too. I had always been a bit of a writer and I now do freelance articles for a national monthly magazine; colour pieces I suppose you would call them, about country life and country people. I very much enjoy it.

***

One evening about a year ago, just before dark, I was coming back into town after visiting an old logger up the river. There were some storm clouds right over my town and just as I reached its outskirts we were hit by a terrific wind. It shook my car – and it's a solid old

Toyota Crown – and then heavy rain began. Visibility was so poor that I was forced to stop.

The wind died after fifteen minutes and the rain eased so I took off again, but it was now quite dark and there were a lot of small branches and pieces of rubbish on the road so I drove very slowly. I took my usual route, which follows the river's edge and avoids the main shopping centre.

In one street something on the bitumen right in front of me flipped over just as I reached it. It looked like a photo, but I was too close to stop in time and ran over it. I pulled up and ran back; my wheels had passed right across it and I thought I'd probably damaged it badly. I put it on the passenger seat.

In my garage I looked at it under a light. It was an old print, showing a seated couple, and my tyre tread marks across it were very obvious; there were also some small tears. I left it propped up on my bench to dry out.

Early the next day when I looked at it again I could see that in fact it wasn't too badly damaged and from the little knowledge I had gained at the local newspaper office, where I had seen what they managed to achieve with old prints, I thought it could probably be restored.

From the clothing of the people in this photo it would seem to have been taken in the 1930's – there were similar era photos in my parents' albums. This couple looked to be in their mid-twenties. The man was strongly built, fair haired with a smiling open face – a likeable face. She was slim, perhaps slight, with dark hair pulled back in a bun or perhaps a roll. Not very pretty but – something there – a quality. She had small but bright dark eyes. A married couple, or engaged perhaps.

The two were sitting almost a metre apart, half turned towards each other but looking at the camera. He was in a dark suit and she in a longish dark dress with a narrow fur stole; she was also wearing a corsage.

It was a studio shot, with the backdrop of a nineteenth century street scene – lampposts and horse-drawn vehicles – and, further back, some houses and trees. I turned it over; nothing on the back but the numbers 148/39.

I imagined the photo had come from one of the houses near where I found it, blown through an open window perhaps. It did not look as if it had ever been stuck into an album, but it was in such good condition – or had been before this misadventure – that I thought it was probably valued.

Mid-morning I went back to the street, thinking there might still have been other photos around, and they might have had names on them. There were none, and in fact the whole area had been so completely tidied up by the Council that one would not have known there had been a blow. I looked at the houses and front gardens for some clue but gained nothing.

Two days later our local paper featured eye witness reports and many photos of damage. There were quite a few entries in the 'Lost and Found' column and I decided I would add a "found" to the next edition, leaving my phone number. There was no response, but I decided to run it for a few editions; I had the feeling that this photo would have been highly valued by its owner.

After the photo had dried out I propped it up on my roll top desk; I found I was growing accustomed to it. I was being drawn to its elements – the open and smiling face of the man and the more serious face of the woman. She wasn't that severe I decided; in the way that people like to say there is the hint of a smile on the face of the Mona Lisa I was beginning to fancy there was something similar in the expression of this woman.

While I worked at my desk I found I often looked up at the photo and eventually the thought of someone claiming it brought a pang. I took my own photograph of it, against that day.

After a month and no response I decided it was now finders keepers and I took it to a local studio that advertised a restoration service. The manager said that if we knew which studio had put the numbers on the back it would be better to go back to them; they might even have the original negative. He said he thought it had probably been shot in a Melbourne studio and that some of them kept negatives for many years.

I rang someone I knew at "The Age", a photographer I had met when he came up to the Murray to cover a Royal tour. He said that he had some good contacts because he often used the archives of private studios to illustrate a historical story; why not send it down?

I did this and after a week he left a short phone message to say that he thought it could be a Rogerson Studio production and that he was taking it there. The next morning a Mr. Rogerson rang with both good and intriguing news. They did have the original negative – he had found it from the identifying number – and he had done another quick print, but the woman on the right hand side in *my* print was *a different person.*

"The original was taken on the 14th of May 1939, a Mr Charles Lampe and a Miss Ruth Parmenter."

"Well, how...?"

"I've thought about that." Rogerson had a low quiet voice, that of an old man, but it now went up in pitch. "Mr. Cusack..."

"Phil"

"Leo. This is quite extraordinary – I wish you were looking at this print with me..."

While he had been talking I had taken down the copy I had made. I told him this.

"Oh good. Now the woman in the original photo I am looking at is blonde and much more – buxom, shall we say. Pretty too."

"But it's the same backdrop?"

"Yes, oh yes. Your lady is in our studio alright."

"So – what...?"

"What I'm saying is that this is a print from two different photographs that have been re-photographed."

"It's a forgery!?"

"Well, it's a *composite*. We do this all the time now, on request. Families want us to, say, put photos of their children together."

"Yes but this is... not the same."

"No. It's – irregular, to say the least."

"But why doesn't it have your identifying number on the back of the woman – *my* woman – if it was taken there?"

"Well, she is on the right hand side of the shot, and we always put our numbers on the back of the left hand side, and that's obviously gone."

"Yes, you couldn't ...but wait a minute, if the photo I sent you is a composite – a *new* production as it were – how come the number on the back of the photo of the original couple is still there?"

" Oh yes, you're right" he said, and I heard him turn the print over. "Oh!" – and I heard some fumbling – "because – because – *we* didn't put it there." There was excitement in his voice. "I've just looked at it under a magnifying glass. It's in jet black ink and we always use one with a slight purple cast. I'd missed that."

"But it *looked* right?"

"Yes. Whoever did this, copied the style of our numbering perfectly."

After our phone call I looked more closely at my own copy of the damaged print. Leo Rogerson had told me the cut in the original must have been made along the vertical provided by the lamp post in the middle of the backdrop. I put a strong light on the print to see if I could detect anything but no, it had obviously had been done expertly.

Leo had said he was quite confident he could restore the print I damaged and I asked him to also do for me a print of the original photo – of the *first* couple – but now this news rekindled my desire to meet the local owners; if they did not know about the 'forgery' then I had a story to tell them, but if they *did* know they might have an interesting story to tell *me*.

Driving again down the street where I had found the print – a street of large old houses – I slowed at the spot. All was serene and quiet – an upmarket part of our town in its midday snooze. Silence – almost: just the faint sound of a piano.

On reaching a small shopping centre nearby I checked if it had one of those neighbourhood notice boards – advertising lost dogs, a child's bed for sale, that sort of thing – and it did. I made an A4 sized copy of my photo and pinned it up, with my phone number. Two days later I received a call.

"Yes its mine." The voice that of an old woman. Would I drop by?

***

" PIANO LESSONS. BEGINNERS TO ADVANCED. MISS F. RICKARD" said the sign near the front gate. The house was an attractive wide fronted brick colonial, and the garden was large and neat. A garden maintenance van was parked in the driveway and I could hear a mower. I went up the two steps onto the verandah and pressed a brass button; a two note chime sounded inside and quite quickly the door was opened.

"Mr. Cusack." A 'proper' accent, a smile and a hand offered ; a small, very old woman, immaculately dressed, hair swept up and perfectly in place. I did not offer 'Phil' because I felt that it would probably remain 'Miss Rickard'.

I followed the diminutive figure down a long wide hallway and into a large room that itself opened through French windows onto the rear garden. I could see a young man on a ride-on.

The walls of the room were covered in framed photos and there were many more on desks and shelves. There were two little tables overflowing with sheet music and a grand piano; the top of it also supported many more small framed photos.

I had brought a print of the photo I had taken – I had already told the woman I was having the damaged one restored – and as she sat on a chaise and invited me to sit in a leather armchair opposite I handed the envelope across.

She opened it quickly, glanced inside then looked up and smiled. It hit me – *this* was the woman in the photo – sixty, no seventy years on – but definitely the one. Her eyes were the clincher – dark and round and bright – still bright.

"I should be able to bring you your print in a week's time." I did not say that I had originally been hoping that no-one would claim it; she might have found that a bit odd. "I felt that as I was the one who had damaged it I should fix it up."

"Well thank you very much. It's very good of you."

"That's you in the photo?"

She nodded.

"And was that your..." I didn't know how to finish the question, especially as I now knew some things.

She nodded, and then asked me if I would take some tea.

When she had left the room I stood up and began to look at the many photos on the walls. Some were recent, showing her with, I assumed, her pupils – still teaching, yet she must have been in her nineties!

There were several photos on one wall that showed groups of young people and these looked as if they were from the same era as the print. I looked at these more closely and found first my hostess and then the young man; had it been a social club, or a church group?

Frieda Rickard came in with the tea things and saw what had taken my attention.

"Ah you've found us, Monsieur Poirot."

"I've found you, and I think..."

"Charles? Yes he's there. We were in the same church group. In Caulfield. We used to go on a lot of outings."

"Did you – become engaged?"

She nodded but did not go on. Then she took a deep breath, as if coming to a decision, and said that the damaged photo was taken just before the War and that Charles had been killed in North Africa. She did not seem inclined to say any more about that.

She told me that she had moved here from Melbourne after the War, bought the house and had taught in it ever since.

"Over a thousand pupils." She chuckled. "Slowing down a bit now."

"Well you're..."

"Ninety four."

"That's – incredible."

"Good genes I suppose." Her eyes – they really were bright – crinkled. "But I don't do Rachmaninov any more."

We small talked but my mind was on what Leo Rogerson had told me, that the photo was a composite. Someone – she? – had replaced the image of one young woman with an image of herself.

I silently willed her to talk about this but she did not. She spoke of other things, remaining calm and self-possessed. I was sure she believed I was ignorant of the forgery and somehow the idea of revealing what I knew seemed too harsh a thing for me to bring up. She was so old, and the photos were taken so long ago; let it be.

At the front door though, as I was promising to ring her when the restored print arrived, and she was continuing to be so "grateful" – so *gracious* – a little bubble of irritation rose within me. I decided to throw a pebble onto that calm surface.

"Oh, I didn't mention. My friend in Melbourne managed to find the studio that you went to in 1939." I saw her stiffen. "Yes. The owner of the place, still one of the Rogersons – he's the one doing the job. He talked with me; he was quite excited about it."

I walked to the front gate and as I shut it after me I glanced back at the house; Frieda Rickard had not moved and was looking down at me with an intense gaze.

***

A week went by and when I returned from a trip one day there was a phone message from the woman. She said that as she hadn't heard from me she assumed that the restored print had not yet arrived but she was wondering if I might like to drop by for a drink later that afternoon – say six o'clock? I phoned and said yes.

I was intrigued; was she now inclined to reveal to me the truth about the photo? Or did she just want some adult relief from a succession of young students? Even without the magnet of the mystery I would have been interested in a talk with her. Frieda Rickard was exactly the sort of person who could provide good copy for an article – an old, intelligent person living in a country town, and in full possession of her faculties. And there was also the chance "a drink" meant something stronger than tea.

When I arrived I could hear piano and I guessed a lesson was still in progress. Instead of interrupting by pressing the button I walked down the side of the house and around into the back garden. There in the shade of a Liquidamber were two cane chairs and a small table with glasses and what looked like bottles of whisky and gin. The afternoon was looking up.

I walked up close to the French window and stood there, thinking this was a discreet way of letting her know I had arrived. Within a minute she came up to the window, smiled and held up three fingers, which I took to mean she would be free in three minutes.

I went for a stroll around the large garden which like the front one was well tended: lawn and trees for the most part. Just behind the low back fence was a public walkway and on the other side of that was the Old Man himself. It was prime real estate, and even in this country town would be worth a million dollars. The house was well screened from any walkers and I could see that there were enough evergreen trees in the garden to ensure this even in winter. I could still hear the piano but then it stopped and I walked back to the drinks table. A minute or two later my hostess came out of a rear door carrying a tray with an ice bucket and a platter of savouries.

I watched her while she poured drinks: was she 'duchessing' me, as perhaps she did the parents of potential students?

As she poured the drinks – a whisky and ice for me and a gin and tonic for herself – she gossiped about the student who had just left, but in a 'safe' way; she mentioned no name, and I was sure she knew I hadn't seen him or her. She told other stories, about ex-students, and very entertainingly: amusing and insightful. I felt she could well yield a good article, if she felt so inclined.

She looked down a lot while she talked, in remembering pose, but she also looked at me a good proportion of the time. It was that same bright intense gaze; her eyes had not lost the lustre that was in the photo taken when she was in her twenties. This to me was very unusual; it has been my observation that people's eyes lose their brightness as they age. Also, eyelids tend to droop, and pouches appear, but not in this lady. Had she been one of my town's older 'socialites' I might have suspected cosmetic surgery.

Her gaze, when I received it, was so intense that I began to think that she was not just *connecting* with me but *examining* me. *Assessing* me.

She told me that she had read two of my recent magazine articles since meeting me and had enjoyed them. As they had not been published in the local paper I felt this showed some degree of enterprise. I said as much and she shook her head and said simply "Internet". That surprised me.

I slipped into the role of interviewer and she obliged with her history. Born in Melbourne in 1915 in what sounded like pretty comfortable circumstances – father with a wholesale trading business in the city, big house on Dandenong Road: a chauffeur. She had not trained for work; "Father thought it 'unnecessary'."

She had become a skilled pianist. "I played at amateur concerts, at private parties, at balls – at what we called soirees – but I was not top drawer. I realised by the time I was twenty five and had been to a lot of recitals that I was not that good.

Good enough to teach others, up to a certain level. What do they say, 'those who can, do, those who can't, teach'". A wry smile, but not, I would have said, bitter.

"My father died in1943 and after the war I decided I would like to make a big change. I'd been up here on holiday and liked it; bit hot in summer but I loved the river and the atmosphere. I had the idea that in a country town of this size I could support myself by teaching piano. I brought my mother with me."

I was intrigued; no mention of Charles. "That was a big move. Gutsy!"

"Not as 'gutsy' as you might think" One could hear the quotation marks; not a word she would normally employ. "Father had left me quite a lot of money. I didn't really *have* to earn a living; if it hadn't worked out we could have gone back to Melbourne. But it did, and mother liked it here too. She died in 1953, in this house.

I have always been able to space out my lessons so that they are not too taxing. And in the early years I had a very full social life – race meetings and balls and tennis parties, you know. I was on *the list*." The wry smile again; think the actress Judy Davis.

"No – *particular* friend...?"

She nodded. "Yes, a couple, but – how shall I say – you are a bold inquisitor Mr. Cusack – I realised that I no longer wanted to get married. I had no interest in children – not in having my own. I liked the young students, especially if they were keen and had talent, but I was also glad that they could go home to someone else." She looked at me. "Something missing perhaps."

It was a challenging look. Was she daring me to confront her with what I knew?

"Charles...?" I said it tentatively. Gently really; I was by now fairly certain that it was she who had altered the photo – but had she hurt anyone? Wasn't it really only her own business?

She shook her head. "No, I mean within me," and she placed her small hand over her heart. "But yes, if Charles..." She fell silent.

"He was killed you said in Africa?"

"Yes, but..." She looked down and was silent again, and this time I thought looked distressed. The change was alarming. Then her head snapped up, as if she had made a decision. Her eyes were still bright, but now they glistened.

"Did Mr. Rogerson tell you anything about that photo?"

'Yes." And I added "Everything."

She turned away, looking towards the house, her face now in profile to me.

"Look' I said, "It's entirely none of my business. Let me just bring you the photo when it arrives. I've upset you. I'm sorry."

"No, it's alright. It's good. I've lived with that fabrication far too long." She looked me full in the face. "I'm glad of that wretched storm – I'm glad it was you that found it." And then she told me all.

***

She had joined the Fellowship group at the local church *because* she was attracted to Charles. He was a couple of years younger than she and different from her, she said, in many ways: very good at sport, warm, friendly, open, and easy going.

"Opposites do attract Mr Cusack. At least *I* was attracted to him – but he was spoken for. I didn't know that when I joined the group; everyone else did!"

"Ruth Parmenter."

"Ruth, yes. But I hoped he would notice *me*. We do that don't we – did that happen to you? I hoped I could steal him away. Surely on one of our trips to Bendigo or the Dandenongs or Geelong he would find he liked my company? When I played the piano in one of the restaurants we visited or one of the halls, wouldn't he be impressed?"

"I can't see you as ' the other woman'."

She laughed. "You're right. I must have been hopeless. I don't think it even registered with him that I was interested. Ruth knew of course, but she always remained so nice to me – I think she could see I was no threat to her. And she was all the things young men

109

like; she was pretty and could dance and had a nice figure. And she was *blonde*! What chance did I have? Plain and dour."

"You're not plain and dour to me."

"Thank you. Anyhow they got engaged early in 1939. Ruth brought along the studio photo of the two of them and I asked her where it was done and went and ordered a copy.

Foolish – but it was such a good likeness of Charles and I was losing him and it would be something nice to keep. My heart was broken of course. I intended to cut the photo in two or fold it over or something. They asked me to the wedding but I couldn't bear to go.

I didn't do anything with the photo and then Charles was killed in the War. That's when I decided to do – what I'm sure you know I did."

I nodded. "You went to the same studio."

"Yes, but it wasn't as simple as that. I studied and studied the photo to make sure I would be sitting in exactly the right position, with the same backdrop of course."

"They must have thought it strange, that you wanted to be on the right hand side of a picture. With nobody on the left?"

"They did. I said it was to be used in a theatrical production and they accepted that."

"How did you know the photo could be cut so exactly, so it was undetectable?"

"I had already taken the print to another studio and told them I was interested in cutting it that way – didn't tell them the reason. They said it would cut perfectly along the vertical lamp post. And then after I sat for *my* photo I took it to a *third* studio to have it done. Covering my tracks you see."

"You were very thorough."

"Yes, perhaps I missed my calling. But you have found me out."

"Yes – 'One dark and stormy night'. How did it get onto the street?"

"I had been looking at it on the front verandah, with a few other photos. It was still loose – I'd never had it framed. Well I couldn't really have it on a wall, someone from those days might have seen it."

"Surely not after all this time? Up here?"

"No, I suppose not – but it is a lie – *my* lie – and I wanted to keep it hidden."

Her story reduced us now to silence. After a minute she smiled again, a soft and somewhat tired smile." I'm a weak and wicked woman."

She put the two prints on a small table near the French windows in her music room and we looked at them together. One of her hands was on the table between them and I noticed it was trembling slightly. I had an urge to reach across and squeeze it but stifled the impulse; we were still then 'Mister Cusack' and 'Miss Rickard'.

***

She did agree to be the subject of one of my articles. I interviewed her in two long sessions – she said she found the first one exhausting – but she was great. For the finished article I received a bonus fee and a special letter of thanks from the editor of the magazine. I took a bottle of good Scotch round to her and we toasted our achievement.

As I was leaving on that occasion she said "Did you tell me that you had developed – for some reason unfathomable to me – a liking for that photo?"

"I did. I have."

"Then it's your's," and she went to fetch it.

I accepted it. And I felt I understood.

"Moving on?"

"Yes. Never too old."

***

I call and see Frieda Rickard every so often – it has been Phil and Frieda for some time now – and we enjoy a good talk under that Liquidamber with a drink or two. We have become friends.

And that print? It sits for now propped up on my roll top desk. After she dies I think I will have it framed and put on the wall of our dining room. Then if conversation with new dinner guests ever flags I can say; "See that photo there. See anything unusual about it?" – and I can tell them a good story.

TEN

THE BOY AT THE YARDS

When he told Susie he intended to go down to the saleyards she had objected – as he thought she would. "It will be very cold Dad – they're saying there'll be a frost. You're supposed to keep warm now you know." He didn't say that he thought that there mightn't be many more opportunities, the way he was feeling some days.

Bernie would pick him up at five and they should be back by ten, he said; he promised he would rug up. They would have some breakfast at the canteen – if he had any appetite.

Susie had said no more, though he knew she wasn't happy. She was a wonderful girl – and she had a good husband in Trev; it had been wonderful of them to take him in, as soon as the diagnosis had been confirmed.

***

He'd always loved the sounds and the smells of the saleyards, from the time he'd got his first job there at fifteen. He'd loved it really from before then – when he'd gone there with his father to deliver some weaners or steers, or to buy some replacement breeders. When they'd sold the farm and moved into town he'd still gone down to the yards

What he liked especially was not so much the auction but the preparation for it – the movement and the noise. He knew that to a casual visitor it might have seemed like chaos – men shouting, gates clanging and cattle going this way and that along the lanes, seemingly at random; how did the poor animals know where to go? But the men knew – and before he was twelve years old he had decided that one day he would join that band of men.

He could still remember that first day on the job; he had ridden his bicycle to the yards – these same yards. That had been in winter too; his mother had bought him a pair of leather gloves and a thick brown top – brown because it wouldn't show the stains from mud and cattle manure she'd said. He had a new beanie too, bright blue, knitted especially by his aunt Ruth, a generous one to accommodate his mop of hair. His father had lent him his torch.

He had been asked to be there by five; he'd left the house at four and was at the yards by four-fifteen. Pitch black – and a fog that morning coming in off the river. There was no-one else there, and after a few minutes of waiting he went down to the first holding pen and brought up some cattle to the drafting yard. He knew the cattle – some of Charlie Swinson's Angus steers. There were forty of them, too many to fit into just one of the selling pens, so he had divided the mob into two and parked them in two of the nearest selling pens, ready for someone – himself probably – to take them to their correct ones.

Still no-one had arrived so he had brought in the next group, fourteen cows and calves. He drafted the cows off the calves and made up two more pens. He was about to get a third mob when he heard someone coming along one of the lanes – Alec, the agency's head stockman.

"Oi young Smith, you're doing me out of a job" he accused, but good naturedly. He checked the cattle. "That's good. Take those steers to – " and he held a clipboard up to the small overhead electric light he had switched on – " J 13 and 14, then put the cows and calves into the first two pens of L and then open up D 7."

He'd bustled the cattle along to their pens and run back; Alec was not quite ready for him. "Cripes, you're gonna make me work Smithy" – he remembered everything that was said to him that day – "you little skinny guys are always quick."

He *was* little – five feet six in the old language – and thin too in those days. 'Wiry' some people said – he did put on muscle as the years went by. That was falling off him these days, the thing had such a grip on him; he couldn't bring himself to look now in the bathroom mirror.

He still had a good head of hair though – grey now, but once it had been jet black. That was what they'd called him at school – "Black": black hair, and eyes so dark they too often looked black. The Irish in him, some people said.

***

Bernie was right on time, as he'd known he would be. The man was old agency too, and knew all about being on time and in the right place. Bernie and he had started at the yards the same year. When he had been promoted to an inside job in the agency store up in the town Bernie had been transferred to another town along the river at the same time, also to an inside job.

He had still managed to get down to the yards sometimes for a while on sale days, in his lunch hour, or early in the morning before his proper job. When he talked to Bernie on the phone he'd hear that he was doing the same thing – "Beryl reckons I'm pitiful" – but he'd admitted that his Shirley had said much the same thing to him. But good naturedly, as if to say "everyone has to have something;" well, she'd had her card parties.

Bernie and he had retired in the same year, and after his friend had come back to their home town they'd gone down to the yards together at least once a fortnight. They would get there early in the morning and "supervise" the drafting and penning up. After that job was done and before the actual auction began they would go to the canteen for egg and bacon rolls and coffee, and yarns with the stockmen. It was like their second home; "their real home" Shirl had said.

As he sat now beside Bernie as they travelled in the old Vauxhall, warm and comfortable, he was scarcely listening as his friend relayed his latest "news". Well, Bernie was always talking – talk the leg off an iron pot people used to say – and you didn't really have to listen, or say anything in reply. But this morning he also felt a detachment – a *distance* – as if he were cocooned. It was quite a nice feeling.

They pulled up at the front of the yards under the single light; they could see two other lights on at the rear, over the drafting yards, and could make out a man standing on a rail, waving a stick and talking – shouting probably. They couldn't hear him from within the car but when they got out they could. Then they heard another sound – the familiar click and clatter of hooves in one of the nearer lanes, and soon they saw a small group of Shorthorn heifers coming along, followed by a stockman on foot. He was well dressed for the cold, in a brown fleecy top and a beanie. He was small and slight, and looked very young, and he waved to them as he went past.

They went down to the drafting yard; Tom knew them both. "G'day Fred. G'day Bernie. By gee you're soldiers – morning like this", then "I've got a new assistant this morning – first day on. Keen as mustard; I think he'll be good. Better not let him hear that of course."

Bernie started talking again but once more his voice seemed to come from far away. Even the sounds of the cattle drafting were muted. There was a kind of hush – but not quite – there *was* a sound – a sort of hum. He couldn't tell where it was coming from – or maybe it was coming from *him*. It was rather nice; it made him feel peaceful.

The sound of boots on bricks cut through and there again was the young stockman beside them, putting one foot up on the bottom rail of the yard. At that moment Tom was having a little difficulty in the drafting yard with a couple of beasts. "Do you want me in there?", the boy already half-way up the fence before Tom waved him back. Keen – like I was he thought. He looked directly at the newcomer and got a quick smile in return from a dark-eyed alert face. The lad whipped his beanie off to scratch his head for a moment, revealing a shock of black hair.

The gate opened and the cattle rushed out, the lad following them up the lane, and he turned to watch them. A light had been switched on further along the lane and as the little procession passed under it the blue beanie stood out. It's like a star he thought – and the strange but soothing hum returned.

He watched the star until it disappeared and then he took gentle hold of his friend's arm. "Bernie, I'm sorry – I think have to go back home."

ELEVEN

THE BEQUEST

M y neighbour has a beef cattle stud and is an active promoter of his breed. He exhibits his cattle at shows, and is now on the council of his breed society.

A month ago when he dropped in for a yarn he mentioned that he had just received the agenda for the next meeting of the council and that it contained an item that was bound to cause heated debate; a very large sum of money had been offered to the society – but some of the councillors would find difficulty in accepting it. Max admitted that he himself did not yet know which way he would vote.

A hundred thousand dollars were being offered from the estate of a recently deceased member of the society – to be invested – and the interest earned to be spent on a prize for the champion bull at our annual Royal Show. The problem for the councillors lay in the fact that the member had fallen from grace six years before his death, and over a bull that he himself was exhibiting at the Royal; it was believed that he had cheated over the bull's birth date. Adding to the present difficulty for the councillors was the stipulation *that the prize be named after him*: " The Alf Nicholson Memorial."

My neighbour had told me years before about the incident involving the bull, and about the cloud that had continued to hang over Alf Nicholson's name. It was all the more interesting to both of us in particular because the man and his wife lived in our district here on the Murray.

 I had met Kay Nicholson; she is a member of my wife's craft group and has twice been to our place. She is I would say by far the wealthiest woman in the group – owner of the largest and most valuable property around – drives a late model Bentley – but I found she gave herself no special airs. From the short conversations I had had with her I gained an impression of intelligence and balance – a person of real substance. But I had never met her husband.

***

The events of six years ago as I understood went like this: the Nicholsons had a bull in one of the classes at the Royal – let's say 'age eighteen to twenty months'. By all accounts it was a magnificent animal, already a champion at several country shows before reaching the Royal.

Breeders of stud cattle have to submit a record of details about their new calves with their breed society – sire and dam and birth date. It is the breeder's responsibility to enter that birth date as accurately as possible. To knowingly enter a false date, and especially to bring it forward by say several months – that is, to maintain that the animal is much younger than it is – is regarded almost as a crime.

My next door friend has admitted that there is a natural temptation to fudge the birth date, especially if one has a calf that is a cracker, and that could be in the running for a show championship one day. A bull recorded with an incorrect birth date competes against bulls in his age class on an unfair basis; because he is actually older than his classmates he is likely to be bigger and to look more impressive.

And if he wins his class he can then go on to compete against the winners of the other age classes for the championship.

It is the easiest thing for a breeder to record an incorrect birth date, and if done carefully, no-one would ever know. The temptation to bring that birth date forward is one to which, Max assures me, *he* has never yielded.

This particular bull of the Nicholsons had been winning championships at our regional shows in the lead-up to the Royal, but because the animal looked so much bigger and more mature than its competitors some of the other exhibitors had become suspicious. However, as the date of birth which featured in the shows' catalogues was the one already accepted by the breed society, from the calving records submitted by the breeder, they felt they could do little.

Some of those exhibitors were on the council and they passed on their suspicions to the man who would be judging at the Royal; at that show he too quickly formed a doubt – and acted. He put the animal right down the end of the line-up – in effect, last.

In his address to the spectators at the conclusion of his placings he said that at first glance he thought the bull was very attractive but he had decided that it was *too extreme* for its age – in size and muscle development – and that its progeny would probably be unsuitable for the general meat trade in this country. "We do not need animals like that in the breed", he said.

It was clever; he had avoided calling Alf Nicholson a cheat – thus also avoiding the possibility of a libel suit – but had removed the animal from serious contention, for the class ribbon and thus for the eventual championship.

Max tells me the word quickly spread amongst the society's members as to the real reason for the action of the judge, and Alf Nicholson himself seemed to realize what had happened. He stopped exhibiting – stopped going to society meetings – and no longer took an active part in any of the society's activities; Max said he became reclusive, spending all of his time on "Yannowie".

He did begin his own on – property auction sale of bulls two years later. These sales have been only moderately successful; none of the big and established stud breeders attend, despite the fact that the man is offering for sale some of the best of the breed. I am not a stud breeder but I have been to able to afford to buy a bull there, just to put into my commercial herd.

***

There were to be only three of these annual sales before the man developed cancer, and within a year he had died; that was three months ago. His widow has not been to our place since that time; she continues to live on "Yannowie", and, I have heard, intends to manage the considerable enterprise herself.

***

Max said he was at a loss as to which way to vote on the bequest; a hundred thousand dollars would provide for such a generous prize that it would put those offered by other breed societies in the shade – a lovely advertising point in the very competitive world of stud cattle breeding – but *should* the councillors, knowing the history, accept it?

I found myself intrigued; why would a man like Alf Nicholson risk his good name by falsifying the birth date of one of his bulls? Winning a Royal Show championship was a very prestigious thing, yes, but was it worth risking one's reputation? It did not add up, in my eyes.

***

I asked Max what he knew of Alf Nicholson; very little, he said. I said that perhaps he should find out – go and see Kay Nicholson at least. It might help him to come to a conclusion; I thought to myself it might even lead him to the belief that the man had *not* tried to mislead – that he might have made an honest mistake when doing the progeny records – even possibly that there *was* no mistake, and that the stated birth date was genuine. Even amongst my own cattle a calf is born now and then that grows much faster than his brothers and sisters.

Max said he just did not have the time to do some investigating though he would love to do it, and somehow I found *myself* offering to do it. I am semi-retired here – we have a man who does nearly all that needs to be done on the farm now; I would have the time and, as said, I was intrigued. What might I find out?

Also, an unbidden thought had entered my mind; could this offer have been Alf Nicholson's way of *getting back* at a group of people who had effectively shunned him? It was certainly a nice conundrum he was putting them in, one that would cause difficulty and possibly some embarrassment.

***

Because I knew Kay Nicholson, and I was bound to end up talking to her, I thought the best way to start was to see her. Max thought I should speak to the stud groom first; "they don't miss anything" were his words.

Paul Foster wasn't hard to find; stud grooms apparently tend to *remain* stud grooms. With just one phone call Max found out where he was now working.

***

"See – I never saw the calf at birth." Paul said. "He was dropped in one of the back paddocks and Mister Nicholson said because there was plenty of good green feed out there we could forget about bringing them in for a while. And we were building extensions to the yards near the house so we were really busy. Mister Nicholson said he'd take care of recording the birth dates of any calves in that

123

paddock. He used to go out there on a four wheeler – used to go all over the place on it. He was always looking at the cattle."

"So when you saw the calf...?"

"He was huge – much bigger than the others. He looked about twelve months old, but Mister Nicholson said he was only six. Lachlan and I thought he must have made some mistake – got the dates mixed up."

"So you didn't believe Alf Nicolson?"

"Well – you have to don't you? I mean" and he gave an embarrassed grin," he's the boss."

"But I know people do fudge birth dates Paul."

"Yeah – but no one does it by that much. I think he just made a mistake."

I asked him what he had thought of Alf Nicholson generally and he said he'd found him a good boss – very careful with money but not mean – fair – and completely honest.

"If there was something wrong about that bull's birth date it was just a mistake of his."

"And it *could* have been correct?"

"Yes, it could have been. You do get the odd freak."

I located Lachlan, Paul's assistant at the time; he too was still working as a groom.

"It was me that had the real problem with the bull. My girlfriend and I were living in a cottage right near the yards and we kept the future show bulls in a paddock next door. I could see them all the time. They use to come right up to the fence for a scratch. We had two other bulls the same age as Emperor – well, supposed to be – but he was much bigger and older looking. It just didn't seem possible that Mister Nicholson had got it right."

He said it was probably he that started the action. He told his partner of his worries, she confided them to a friend of hers at a show, who told her boyfriend, who was a groom on another property, and he mentioned it his employer.

"I did bring it up with Mister Nicholson. He laughed it off the first time; I said I was worried he had made a mistake but he had this little paddock book he always carried and showed me the note he had made but I was still worried about *what people would think*. I suggested another time that even though the birth date was right that he should *make* it a bit earlier – make it *look* better. He only laughed at that; Paul did too – said he'd never heard of such a thing. But I think that's what he should have done."

When I drove away from talking with Lachlan I asked myself if I was any the wiser. Neither of the men had actually witnessed any wrongdoing – and both of them had attested to the man's general honesty and good character. And the calf could well have been "a freak." And if it were not, Nicholson might just have just made a mistake. But – of that magnitude...?

***

The two young men had talked to me about Alf Nicholson the employer and wealthy landowner. I had an urge to talk to someone who had known him before he had reached that position. I remembered that his wife had told me both he and she had grown up in a little town just west of Swan Hill and that Alf's first job was with the Swan Hill branch of one of our national livestock agencies.

I phoned the manager of the branch there and asked if he thought there would still be anyone who would remember Alf. He said that the man who was the manager at the time Alf was there as a teenager still lived in the town. It is only a two hour drive there from my place and I went up straight away.

Jack Pringle must be nearly ninety but he is in very good health, and with an excellent memory. He was more than happy to talk about my subject; I hardly needed to ask a question.

"Alf Nicholson was the best employee our firm ever had. If we'd had more like him...

He was full of beans – and very capable with stock. My goodness he had a good eye. You know, he was the youngest fellow we had on the staff – and we used to have a big staff then – but clients would make a point of asking for him, if they wanted someone to go out to their farm and help them draft up their sale sheep.

He was just as good with cattle too. And he was spot on with values. I noticed that very quickly – after a little while even our auctioneers asked Alf what he considered a fair price. And of course it didn't take him long to work out what we all knew – there's easier and quicker money to be made *trading* livestock than breeding and growing them.

He was only here a year – what was he, sixteen – seventeen – when he asked me if he could do some dealing himself – privately. I said no – we've got to be seen to work for our clients, I told him. It gets tricky if you are buying for yourself – conflict of interest. He said he understood – but I knew I had a live-wire, and I kept a closer eye on him.

He was living with an aunt here – his mother's sister – and her son had a small block just out of town. I noticed that the son started to buy pens of sheep and cattle at our sales. I guessed that Alf and the cousins were in cahoots; Alf was doing the buying but using the other one's name. He'd put them on the place for a while and then flog them.

You know yourself you can sometimes buy pens really cheaply and sell them again a few weeks later for a profit. Sheep and cattle prices go up and down all the time – and they vary from one place to the next. You can buy here one day, truck them straight down to Bendigo and get more for them the next.

Anyhow – I didn't stop young Nicholson. All of us have done a bit of the 'extra' at times – and he was doing it very carefully. But then the little place next to Alf's cousin came on the market and blow me down Alf bought it. At—what – eighteen! He must have spun the bank manager a good yarn – or maybe the aunt went guarantor. And then the cousin decided to sell his own place a year later and Alf bought that!

That was the end of Alf working for us. He was only twenty but he must have reckoned he had enough land to become a full time trader. I was really sorry to see him go. Course we still saw a lot of him – in and out of the yards all the time – coming into the office to see if we knew someone wanting to sell or buy. And boy, didn't he do well."

Jack Pringle gave me the name of another old-timer, an ex-policeman, who still lived in the town and who had had quite a lot to do with the young Alf Nicholson. The man was not as spry as Jack but his memory was as good; both men were wonderful 'interviewees'.

"Yes I suppose I got to know Alf pretty well", Mick Lloyd said. "Before I met him I had *heard* of him of course because he was the biggest dealer around here. By far.

It was part of my job then to see if men who were moving stock had the right papers, and time after time I'd find that if I pulled up a drover or a truckie his sheep or cattle belonged to Alf Nicholson. Upriver or downriver – out on the plain – chances are they were doing a job for Alf. He must have had thousands of head on the roads all the time. Think of how much money he must have had tied up. And you know what, I believe it was always *his own money*. I don't think he used a bank overdraft or anything like that. And he always paid in cash!

I talked to him once about that – actually it was the first time I ever met him. I thought I should warn him about carrying so much cash. Everyone knew about it, so he was a set up to be robbed. I thought though that any attempt on him was likely to get messy; Alf wasn't the kind of person who'd hand over his money just because some bloke asked him to – even two or three blokes. Even if they were armed. Alf or someone would end up in hospital. Or the morgue.

I told him that if he had to do it, he should take precautions. He said did I mean carry a gun and I said hell no, I mean take a couple of friends with you. He said he already had a couple of friends and pointed to the back of his ute. Two blue heelers!

He learned to fly, and bought himself a plane, and of course then he was everywhere. I met up with him a lot over – oh – ten years.

He didn't seem to have many friends though – you hardly ever saw him yarning with anyone – and he never went into a pub. He was always on his own – except for those bloody dogs – but sometimes when I came out of the station he'd be there, leaning on his ute – like he was just waiting."

"What did you talk about?"

"Well – that's hard to say. Nothing much really. The weather – maybe I'd tell him something funny I'd seen – you saw a lot of funny things in the job. He never talked about people or any deal he had just done – he might say something about a road or a bridge. It's hard to say *what* we talked about. But I think I was as close to being a friend of his as anybody. Except Kay of course – later.

And *that* was a funny turnout. I had never seen Alf with a girl – I don't think anyone had – and then he ups and marries Kay Potts. Big surprise to everyone – big surprise to *me* – I think it could have been a big surprise to her!"

"Did you know her?"

"Only by sight. She lived about thirty miles out. I think she worked on farms."

"Doing what?"

"Oh – stock work. They were a family that did that – worked for other people."

"So – not well off?"

"No way. She and Alf had the same sort of upbringing – pretty hard."

"And it was about the time they got married that he bought "Yannowie" wasn't it?"

"That big place? Yeah – another big surprise. I mean – Alf Nicholson was *the* dealer. He'd buy a mob of sheep one morning and sell them that afternoon if there was a profit in it. Then he ups and buys that place – a beauty they tell me – way outside his league most of us would have said."

"He gave the locals *two* things to talk about ."

"Yes – and I can tell you it was talked about for a long time too. Don't know which was the more amazing – him buying that place or getting married." He grinned at me, and then his face told me he had thought of something else. "And then we heard he was going into stud cattle. *Alf Nicholson* – paying thousands for stud bulls!" He shook his head. "He was full of surprises."

"Last thing Mick. Would you say you trusted his word?"

With that the man's demeanour changed; I think I saw the policeman emerge. He looked keenly at me – as if he had just heard a significant thing in an investigation – as if he had just realized that this could be the reason for my visit.

"Well – the way you are asking that – I guess there is something behind it?"

I told him then about the "scandal" involving Alf's name of six years before, and now the bequest and my attempt to arrive at the truth of it.

"Alright – I'll give it to you as straight as I can. From my knowledge of Alf Nicholson over the years I knew him here – he was absolutely straight. A man of his word. Tough in business – he drove a hard bargain, everyone would tell you that – but once he'd agreed on a deal he'd stick to it."

As I was leaving and we shook hands he looked at me seriously; "Alf Nicholson was a decent, honest man".

***

Now, finally, I went to see Kay Nicholson. "Yannowie" is not far from where I live. It's a huge place – magnificent homestead: what real estate agents like to call a 'Signature Property.'

I had told Kay on the phone that a friend who was a councillor in the breed society had asked me to gather more information about her husband so that they could do a good press release when the bequest was announced – a slight lie, but one I thought I could live with. She agreed without hesitation; I wondered if she had been expecting someone to turn up.

She met me on the wide front verandah of the homestead and suggested we have tea out there. A maid brought a tray – a big pot of tea and fresh scones. I told her the names of the men I had interviewed at Swan Hill, and that both had spoken highly of her husband; she said she remembered both.

"Mick said it came as a shock when they learned you had bought this place."

She laughed. "I think Alf gave people a few shocks around then."

She said the owner of "Yannowie" had been dabbling in currency futures and had lost a lot of money. "Somehow everyone knew that – you can't keep many secrets in the country can you?

He had four kids but none of them were interested in running the place – and anyhow the man really needed cash. He was asking a million, which was a lot of money in the early seventies. Plenty of people were interested but no-one had the money and the banks weren't interested in lending then. It was a bad time – wool prices were low and cattle were down.

Alf always dealt in cash you know; he flew down here with six hundred thousand on the seat beside him in the Cessna; the owner almost grabbed the money off him he said."

"A good buy."

"Yes. The bank valued it at ten in 1990. Of course we'd done a lot of improvements by then – the fences and pastures and the sheds. And a heck of a lot of work on the house. The owner had let the whole place get run-down."

I plunged into the subject uppermost on my mind. "Alf's bequest to the society has taken the councillors by surprise. It's so big."

She shrugged and looked out across the paddocks. "This place was valued for probate at twenty-five million. And we have other assets. A hundred thousand was not such a lot. Another cup?"

We chatted a bit about this and that but I was tensing. Max had asked me to see if the councillors could be given some room to move regarding the *purpose* to which the money might be put. He felt that they would be much more likely to accept the bequest if they did not have to memorialise her husband in a Royal championship. But would I get anywhere with this?

"My friend Max" – no need to hide the identity of the councillor I was helping – she would have probably guessed by now – "said the wording of the letter they received from your solicitor mentioned a prize for the Royal Show Champion Bull..."

She smiled. "Not 'mentioned' Stipulated. *And* in my husband's memory."

I felt I was not going to get movement on this. I also felt quite definitely that my being there with her – or a councillor being there – had been pre-ordained.

I plugged on. "I was wondering if that is mandatory. If the council thought that the money could be better employed in some other way, I wonder if – do you have any discretion there...?"

"No – and I wouldn't exercise it anyhow. That was my husband's wish."

"Oh..." I couldn't think what to say next but she forestalled me anyhow.

"It is also *my* wish."

She had been sitting in her chair at an angle to me; now she turned her body – actually shifted on the seat – and looked very directly at me, unsmiling. "He didn't do it you know."

***

The ground under our conversation had shifted. As if we both recognized that we grew silent – as if each was occupied with his or her own thoughts.

And I *was* thinking – thinking that when I met my friend and neighbour Max I would say that I thought an injustice had been done to Alf Nicholson. Nothing I had heard from anyone – the grooms, the old agency man, the ex-policeman and now his widow – pointed to any wrong doing on his behalf. They should not only accept the bequest but, I thought, with humility.

132

And I had questions about the woman sitting with me, such as – was it *she* who was driving this action? Had *she* initiated the gift? Had there perhaps been no wish for a bequest on her husband's mind? Was it Kay Nicholson's idea entirely to employ this device to attempt to rehabilitate Alf's name – a public righting of a wrong that she believed had been done to her husband?

And if so, I wondered, was there some element of *revenge* in this? The offer was aimed at the very people who had wounded her husband. It might not be a large sum of money to Kay Nicholson but it was sufficiently large to be very attractive to a breed cattle society's council – but if accepted, the council and the society would have to live with the name of Alf Nicholson forever, and attached to the most prestigious award any of its members can win.

Someone once wrote "revenge is a dish best served cold", and this "offence" was six years old. If revenge *were* in the mix it would be a cold – and delicious – dish indeed.

***

Kay broke the silence by suggesting a stroll through her very large rose garden; I think she would have remembered my wife's interest in roses, and our attempts to make something nice of them in front of our home. For twenty minutes we talked varieties and black spot and aphids – and then we walked to my car.

Kay told me that Alf had talked of establishing a top stud herd of cattle from the day they moved onto "Yannowie". After fifteen years they felt they were getting enough very good individuals each year to consider competing at shows. They put on a groom and then an assistant – Paul and Lachlan. They started exhibiting at district shows, winning many ribbons and championships, and after three years of that they decided they were ready to tackle the Royal – but although they did well there over several years, winning many age classes, a *championship* – the best in breed – eluded them.

" Size matters when it comes to the broad ribbon; our cattle were of very good quality, but championships tend go to the quality bull that has that extra growth. We always got pipped in that department. Alf never got down about it – but he was determined to win it.

Then Emperor came along. Alf told me about him long before I saw him. He was born in 'Anabranch'. Alf decided that because the feed was so good there he should leave them be for a few months. He used to go out there on his four-wheeler and when he came back he would be full of him. He'd tell me how fast the calf was growing – much faster than the rest – and what good conformation he had, and magnificent breed character. He was the apple of his eye."

She said that when the staff did muster that paddock they couldn't get over how big the calf was. Alf had told her they were even asking him to check his records. He had laughed about that; he showed her the calving book, and the notes he had taken at the time of its birth.

She and he used to go down to the little paddock where the young show potential bulls were run, in the late afternoons, just to see Emperor. "He *was* an outstanding animal. And he had presence – real sire potential."

Emperor won championships at three local shows and then went off to the Royal. Kay said she came down with influenza just beforehand and had to stay home. "Alf promised to ring on his mobile from the show ring."

"When the judge there said what he did Alf was shattered. He didn't even ring me – I did wonder if something had gone wrong. Alf didn't even stay for the rest of the judging; he drove straight home.

I tried to tell him that what had happened didn't mean that much – we still had the bull and he would be a terrific asset in our breeding herd, but it didn't cheer him up. He said that what the judge had said inferred that he had cheated, and now all the other breeders would think that way too.

We've kept on with the stud as you know and started our own sale. Oh, you bought a bull here. But most of the bigger breeders have stayed away. We are 'suspect' you see."

We reached my car."That Royal experience really changed my husband. He found it hard that someone had questioned his integrity – and had done it in front of all those people."

Some young bulls had come up to the fence just on the other side of my car. They looked good, and I complimented her on them.

"Yes, Alf would have been happy with them. You know, he never really dropped that dream of a Royal championship. It was always with him, when he went out through the cows and calves on the quad. I know he was always looking for his champion.

Actually I have an absolute cracker now. Wouldn't it be something if *I* won the first Alf Nicholson Memorial Championship" We both laughed. Wicked.

TWELVE

RIVER OF LIFE

O n a stretch of the highway that connects many of the towns along the Murray Valley a young man and his wife decided to operate their own small service station. The first two years were a struggle.

The highway has been improved and modernized over the years, and some sections have been relocated at a greater distance from the river; their service station was on one of the 'retired' sections. Though their stretch of road was still in good condition, and still well used by the locals, the much heavier through traffic used the new road.

The couple had known that passing traffic would be light but they had banked on Jaimie, a trained mechanic, gettting jobs for his workshop. He did get a little work, but the local farmers tended to do their own regular vehicle maintenance, and take their cars and trucks into town for any major work.

The couple did add a café, with take-aways, which Tracey managed, and that had helped quite a bit, but they still found it hard going. Then, a lucky event – a large almond orchard on the river five kilometres away passed into new ownership; the principal mortgagor of the business had foreclosed. Reg Bolton moved up from Melbourne and took over the running of the orchard himself.

Shortly afterwards the man had called in at their servo and asked Jamie if he had a truck licence – which he did – and would he be interested in taking a load of almonds to Sydney every three weeks or so? Tracey and Jamie talked it over; the money on offer was very attractive, and Tracey assured her husband that she could manage the business for the two days he would be away each time.

They did not own a truck and could not afford to buy one but Jaimie knew of a ten-tonne tipper on a nearby farm which the farmer used only occasionally and which he might be prepared to make available. It was oldish but had low kilometres on the clock and was in very good condition. The farmer was agreeable, and asked such a reasonable fee for each journey that it made the arrangement very profitable.

That move had saved them; not only were they able to cover all payments on loans but they were managing to put something away. Life all round had looked up; now, if Jaimie's older brother Earl could free himself from his farm up the river as he had promised, even for just a fortnight, they would soon be able to take a holiday – their first in four years. They were thinking of having another baby.

***

The only drawback – the one unpleasant thing – was the orchard owner himself, who had revealed a demanding, arrogant personality. Whenever he phoned to say a load was ready he expected Jamie to drop everything else. He had hinted strongly that if Jaimie ever *did* delay it would mean the end of their arrangement – "there are plenty of men would jump at this run you know."

Tracey knew some of the local women who worked on the almond farm and they all said the man was dreadful. She herself thoroughly disliked him, and in truth Jamie did too, but he did his best to put that aside. The trip to Sydney once every three weeks or so was enabling them to get ahead – that was the main thing.

***

It is a sunny day in late October and Jaimie is clearing away some branches that had been blown down in a storm the night before when a car turns off the road into their driveway. Jamie gives the driver a welcoming wave but the driver, an older man, does not return the greeting, does not even seem to look at him. Instead of pulling up at one of the bowsers he drives over to the parking area.

Jamie continues to rake away the twigs and leaves from the fallen branches but notices that the man has not left the car. As he walks past the vehicle with the wheelbarrow he sees that the driver has put his seat back and is resting. Coming back, and seeing that the man has remained in the car, he walks over to it; there is something about the behaviour of the man that strikes him as odd.

"Are you okay sir?"

"Yes thank you, I just need to rest." The voice is deep and strong, however as the man turns his head towards Jamie, he does it very slowly, keeping his eyes closed. "Is my car alright here?"

"No problem – but would you like to lie down for a while? We have a bunk room round the back here for truckies. You're welcome to use that."

"Thanks, I might have to. I don't want to move just yet for a while though." With that the man turns his head to the front, again slowly, and leans back in his seat.

When Jamie goes into their Take-away for a coffee, he tells Tracy about their visitor. "He doesn't seem to want to move."

***

Half an hour later, from beneath a Landcruiser he is working on in the shed, Jamie sees his wife go to the car. The visitor gets out, and the two walk away together around to the back of their shed. The man is unsteady, and rests one hand on Tracey's shoulder.

At lunch time she tells him that the man is having a Meniere's attack.

"What's that?"

"I looked it up on the Net. It's in the ear – permanent, like the herpes that gives people cold sores."

"What's it do?"

"Causes dizzieness. And nausea. His only crops up now and then he said, and generally doesn't last long, a day or so. He was okay when he left home this morning – it can come on out of the blue apparently. He lives back up the river – near where you used to live. He's going to Mildura but right now he can't handle the car. He'll have to stay here tonight darling. His name's Brian Summers."

While working under the Landcruiser again Jamie realises that 'Brian Summers' rings a bell. And he feels that there is something familiar about the man himself – a strong, fit looking individual, perhaps in his fifties. A farmer? One he used to know?

An hour later Jamie goes to the bunkroom. He enters quietly in case Summers is asleep but finds him awake. The man turns his head slowly towards his visitor and smiles.

"I'm a bloody nuisance."

"Not at all. My wife told me about this..."

"Meniere's."

"Is there something we can do for you?"

"Get me a magic carpet. I'm Brian by the way."

"Jamie. Tracey told me you want to get to Mildura."

"Yes – today. I can't drive but – there's a bus goes up there isn't there? I could manage that."

"Yes – over on the highway – but it's gone now. What about tomorrow?"

Summer gives a sort of groan. "Jamie, it's my daughter – she's had a car accident. She's in the hospital – lost a lot of blood. Still unconscious. They don't know if..." His voice tails off.

Jamie doesn't know what to say. "It's a very good hospital there" he manages eventually.

"Look, I'm sure they're doing all they can, but – Chelsea's my only daughter Jaimie, and – and her mother's dead – and – well, you know..."

***

Jamie goes back to working on the Landcruiser but the man's predicament stays with him. What also stays with him is the growing feeling that he *has* had something to do with the man before – and something significant. Then – with a jolt – it comes to him – that morning on the river – twenty years before.

***

It was a still, sunny day in winter, and he and his brother Earl and their father were fishing from their little dinghy, anchored in the middle of a wide reach of the river. They had been in position for an hour, and had already caught two nice Yellowbelly, which they'd put in the little net hanging over the side. No other boat had come past, and they had seen no-one on the banks; they seemed to have the river to themselves.

It had been cold when they arrived but now pullovers and beanies had been removed and thrown into the bow. Jamie had learned how cold the water itself still was though when he had put the fish he caught into the net.

141

By mid morning there were two or three centimetres of water in the lowest part of the boat; their father had said he intended it to turn it upside down in the backyard and fix the leak. All three knew where it was; the boat was old, and there was one plank that moved a little when they stood on it. Their father, a big man, never trod directly on any of the planks but as a precaution always placed his feet on the ribs that ran across them.

***

Another hour and they were eating their corned beef and baked bean sandwiches. Earl reached behind himself from his seat near the bow and pulled out a plastic bottle of water from under the pullovers.

"Would you like a drink, Dad?"

Their father stood from his position in the stern and took a step forward, to take the bottle from his son. He placed his foot as usual on one of the ribs but it slipped off and all his weight went onto one of the planks – the wrong one. It gave a little under his weight and then broke with a loud snap. The man's foot went right through the bottom, up to his calf, scraping the skin.

He swore and pulled his leg up, and as he did water rushed in. Both boys stood up, alarmed. Their father told them to grab the pullovers from the bow and to shove them into the hole; he himself moved to the bow and began to pull in the anchor but when he saw how quickly the water was entering he used his knife to cut the rope. He slipped the oars into place and began rowing towards the bank.

Earl had first tried to plug the hole with just one of the pullovers, but it had gone straight through. He bunched the remaining two and did manage to wedge them in the gap but still the water flooded in.

Their father rowed for a few seconds but the boat was taking in water so fast he realized it wouldn't make it the bank. Jamie and his brother had crowded into the bow but now he told them to swim for it. Both boys were good swimmers, in their year teams at primary school, and the bank was only fifty metres away. He jumped in behind them.

All three freestyled, and covered the first twenty metres within a few seconds, but then Earl called out, alarm in his voice. He had lost his swimming rhythm; his arms were now just hitting the water rather than making strokes. His face was white.

"What is it son?"

"It's so cold! My legs won't work" The boy nearly went under, and the man grabbed him.

"Turn on your back. Just float." Their father began to breaststroke, pushing Earl before him, but the pair had gone only a few metres when Jamie too called out. Their father angled Earl across to him; Jamie grabbed his brother and both boys went under.

The man brought them up again and wrapped his arms around both. He continued kicking, but now found that he too was beginning to cramp.

Earl slipped out of his arms once more and went under. He re-appeared, thrashing, but disappeared again. His father lunged and brought him up, but in the effort he lost his grip on Jamie and he too went under. When an arm appeared again the man grabbed it, and he managed to pull both boys to him again, but they had moved no closer to the bank, and he could feel his own strength beginning to fail. They were in danger of drowning.

Then – a noise – an engine; he swiveled his head this way and that but could see no boat. However the noise grew louder, and then an old utility came into sight, moving slowly along the top of the bank.

Their father shouted as loudly as he could, and risked letting Jaimie go for a moment to wave. The driver braked and jumped from the cab, raced down the bank, and dived into the water. He was a strong swimmer, and reached the trio in just a few strokes.

"Give me the boys" he said, and he wrapped an arm about each and dog paddled to the bank. "I'm okay" called their father, and did manage some forward movement before the man came back for him. He breaststroked, pushing the father in front of him with his chest. "Christ it's cold" he said.

On the bank their saviour ran to the ute and returned with some old blankets. He lit a fire and piled wood on until he had a roaring blaze.

"You're very lucky. I hardly ever come along here; I was looking for a couple of my stray cows." And that had been Brian Summers – the man now lying in their truckies' bunk room.

***

At three thirty Jaimie goes to the shop for a cup of coffee. Tracey has just returned from checking on their guest.

"He's just the same. He said he takes about a day to come good. But he's'desperate to get to his daughter ."

"I know but – can't he drive at all? He'd just be sitting there, looking straight ahead most of the time…"

"No – he gets sick. He said everything moves – sideways, and up and down. Vertigo – it's not safe darling. He said he only just made it here."

Jamie comes to a decision. He tells his wife about that time on the river. "Trace – I'm going to take him up there. In our car."

"Good idea J. I can manage here." Matter of fact, as if she had anticipated his offer.

"We'll be there in four hours."

"Stay with him overnight."

Jamie nods. "I should be back by lunchtime tomorrow."

***

Jaimie goes to the bunkroom and reminds Summers of their previous meeting twenty years before. He tells him what he has decided. The man objects.

"No..." Jamie is firm. " It's happening."

"Well, thank you Jaimie. Thank you very, very much. If I can lie down on the back seat I'll be right. This thing will be gone by tomorrow – maybe even tonight."

***

As Jaimie is throwing some overnight things into a bag he hears the phone ring, and when he leaves the house Tracey tells him Bolton has rung; he has a load ready to go.

"Will you ring him back and tell what I'm doing. Tell him I can take the load tomorrow. I should be out there just after lunch."

Tracey gives him a look – they both know what the man is like – but she goes back inside. Jaimie goes to help Summers from the bunk room.

When they reach the car Tracey is standing beside it.

"That horrible man! He says you have to go straight out. He said that thing again about giving the work to other people."

They know that it is no idle threat. Jaimie turns towards Summers, but before he can say anything the man says "you go Jaimie. Your wife told me earlier that you were doing it tough before you got this work. It's important to you."

"But..."

The man holds up his hand. ."It's okay – I understand. Really. If I can stay here tonight – and just make some calls from your phone...?"

***

Tracey runs Jamie to the nearby farm to collect the truck and they drive back in convoy. The big fuel tanks on the tipper are already full – he keeps them that way because of the short notice he has come to expect from Bolton. He gets his credit card and his sunglasses; he goes once more to the bunk room.

"I'm sorry about this Brian. I hope your daughter..."

"Thanks – but you get on your way lad. You have to look after your own family."

***

Jamie swings the tipper out onto the bitumen and a kilometre on turns onto the gravel road that leads down to the river. He goes through the entrance to the huge orchard – and a hundred metres in he brings the truck to a halt.

Ahead of him he can see the packing shed – can even see Bolton, pacing up and down in front of the shed, stopping now to stare down the driveway at the stationary truck; Jamie can feel the man's impatience.

He takes only a minute to reach his decision, engages first gear and drives forward. Forward because the road is too narrow to allow him to turn around there; he will have do that up near the shed – right beside the waiting man. He knows there will be an explosion of anger but he doesn't care – he just doesn't care.

146

THIRTEEN

FRIENDS

"Who's this?" There was a note in my wife's voice that brought me out of my office to where she was standing in the kitchen, looking out the window.

Our farm is a small one by Australian standards, though about average size for irrigated dairy farms on this part of the Murray – just under two hundred hectares – but the house is situated at the very back of the farm, so we have a long driveway, the best part of a kilometre. It's perfectly straight, only swinging away just before the house, to go round to the yard and then to the milking shed.

The window in the kitchen looks down the length of the drive and what we could see this day was a man walking towards us, and now about four hundred metres away.

I have always been glad our house is situated so far from the road because it reduces the number of nuisance callers. Marlene is glad too because for her it gives some security, if she happens to be at home on her own anytime. Even on this occasion, with me standing right beside her, I could tell she was a little nervous.

Though he was still at a distance I could tell that our visitor was young – something about the energy and bounce of his walk and, the real giveaway, the fact that he was picking up stones from the edge of the road and throwing them at the fence posts.

"Don't worry" I said, "this'll be our boy."

***

I had first seen young Robert at Elsie Jansen's in town a few months before when I was dropping in some eggs. – a big fit looking lad of perhaps eighteen. She told me that he was her nephew; her sister and brother-in-law had had a farm on the other side of the river, but when they sold it to move to Bendigo earlier in the year, their son had been unhappy about leaving, and she and her husband had offered him a home. She had added something about the boy having special needs but I did not have time on that occasion to learn what they were.

On my next visit Robert was in the front yard and we chatted a little. He was very friendly and polite – a very 'young' eighteen year old was my impression.

While I had Elsie on her own I asked her what she had meant by 'special needs'.

"He is delusional Frank."

"What about?"

"Oh, anything. People. Things. And he hears things."

" Voices?"

"Yes."

"Isn't that...?"

"Schizophrenia? It could be, but – they're not sure. He doesn't have those mood swings. He's very even tempered – a lovely nature really. Very gentle, especially with children. And animals."

After that, while I was working around the farm, I found myself thinking about young Robert. What was going to happen to him? He was strong and healthy, seemed quite intelligent; what was to be his future? I told my wife Marlene about him.

***

"I don't know what his future is," Elsie told me on another occasion. "We worry about that too."

"Do you think he could hold down a job?"

"We have tried that. We have friends here who have businesses. But – he loses concentration Frank. It was the same at school. The first two or three years at high school he did very well, but then he gradually slipped. He didn't sit for any of the exams at the end, it wouldn't have been any good." Elsie, usually a cheerful person, looked unhappy. "He doesn't have any friends. None of the kids he went to school with have anything to do with him now. They don't understand him. He really needs friends Frank. Gerry and I aren't enough. My big worry is that he'll have to go into some sort of Home one day."

I brooded about this on and off and then put it to Marlene that we could help, by bringing the lad out to the farm. I knew she would be wary of having a stranger around, especially one that had a mental problem of some kind. Apart from herself, she would be thinking about our two young grand-daughters, who come out from town with their mother quite often.

"He's only eighteen" I said.

"What would we do with him?"

"Just spend time with him. Talk to him, and get him talking to us."

She gave a good-natured snort at this – talking with people is, she reckons, my favourite pastime.

"He could help me with whatever I am doing. He's had a lot of farm experience." I was trying to make a case.

"Well, we must be careful. We can't get too involved."

I put it to Elsie and Gerry Jansen and they were all for it. Relieved, I could see. When I spoke to Robert he was very keen.

"I know where you live Mr. Faulkner."

"I'll come in and pick you up."

"I can easily walk that far."

Fifteen kilometres? I said no, not to do that, I would be glad to come and get him. But here he was, on foot, and the very next day.

***

Our own kids have grown up and left home and it was nice to have someone young around again. And Robert proved to be a very useful offsider to me when I was doing something like carting hay or fixing a fence. He was immensely strong; he could carry two bales of hay at the same time, and could straighten a steel fence dropper across his knees.

I found though that it was not a good idea to set him a task on his own. For instance, if we were doing something and I asked him to go to the shed and fetch an extra tool or something he could be gone so long that I would have to go and look for him. I might then spy him away in some paddock, and when I caught up with him he might tell me, say, that he had been following a goanna. I found he was easily distracted, and particularly by animals and birds.

***

At our time of life Marlene and I no longer do the actual milking, a young sharefarming couple now attending to that. If Robert was working with me somewhere and he saw Roger or Sue bringing in the cows for milking he would just leave me and follow them. The first time, when he had not returned for some time and I went over to the dairy, I found him in the holding yard, walking amongst the cows, stroking them, and singing to himself.

I caught Roger's eye and he smiled and winked; I had earlier told the couple about our new visitor. Robert's behaviour didn't worry them, and it certainly didn't seem to worry the cows. From then on, if Robert were on the farm during the afternoon milking, he would always go to the dairy then.

***

Marlene and the boy and I often just sat in our kitchen and talked. His contributions were mostly about the natural world – the animals and birds he saw on the farm, and in the bush and in town – but he would also say some things about people he knew or saw; often they were people we knew too.

He seemed to categorise people. We realised "nice" ones were people who were pleasant to him, or who seemed to have time for him.

His aunt was "very nice"; Robert said his uncle was 'always very busy', which we thought possibly meant he did not have much time for his nephew.

If Robert said something about a person it was usually just a simple statement; "Mr. McDonald likes to sit out with his chooks" or "Jake Thompson has more budgies than I ever had."

Just occasionally though he would say something that would stop Marlene and me in our tracks: "Mrs. Parker is very unhappy", "Mr. Gregory is a very bad man" and, a really strange one, "Mrs. Jamieson is going to heaven."

Answers soon came; Kitty Parker left her husband , Phil Gregory was charged with embezzlement and arson, and poor Rita Jamieson died .

You can imagine that we found this extraordinary, and it guaranteed that we listened very closely to any thing of that nature that Robert said. Marlene and I would always ask each other if he had said anything curious in the other's absence.

We grew to recognize when something interesting like that was coming; Robert would go quite still, and look intently off into the distance, as if he could *read* something there.

He seemed to have this secret store of knowledge, and would select a piece of it to share with us. Or did *it* select *him?*

It made us apprehensive – well perhaps not so much apprehensive as simply very alert. What, we wondered each time, were we about to hear?

***

Six months of these visits, and then – *a development;* Robert told me, quietly and seriously, that he had a new friend.

"*You* can't see him Frank, but I can."

This was different. "Tell me about him Robert."

"You know the trees along the river?"

We have Red Gum forest right along our stretch of the Murray, on both sides, and in places it is very wide; in the middle of some patches you can hear neither cars on the road, nor boats on the river.

"He lives in there. And – he's the same colour as the trees. Do you know what colour trees are?"

"Well, green-ish."

"No, they're green and yellow and white and grey and black and brown. And there's all sorts of green. Green like a lettuce – or green like this," and he touched my sloppy joe, which is olive.

"Yes that's right, but – what does your friend look like?" By now I've realised – not human.

"I don't think I'm supposed to say. I think he asked me not to tell anyone."

"So he talks to you?"

"Yes."

"What sort of things does he say?"

He went quiet then, as if he'd already said too much about this 'friend'. Something behind me caught his attention and I turned to see the cows being brought in; I was about to lose him.

"I don't remember," Robert said, as he began to walk off.

"Not anything?"

"No, I never remember any of it."

***

"Oh Frank, what can this mean?"

"Well, he *is* delusional we know. This is part of that. It's harmless though. Isn't it?"

"Well, I don't know. I hope so."

***

It was three days before Robert rang again, and I went in to pick him up. As we drove back through the thick patch of forest beside the river he pointed into the trees. "That's where I met my friend yesterday," he said.

"Do you still think he does not want you to say anything about him?"

"No, it's alright now."

At the house I told him I had to go up onto the roof of our hayshed to re-attach some sheets of iron and that it was too dangerous for us both to be up there; he stayed in the kitchen with Marlene.

I came back about three and he went off to the dairy to see his cows. Marlene put a sheet of paper on the table in front of me. "His friend."

On the paper were large coloured dots – dark and light green, brown, cream, grey and black. The collection formed a shape that was something between round and oval, but with a wavering perimeter. I looked up and must have had an odd expression on my face because my wife laughed. "I know."

I looked down at it again. "What are these little wriggly lines near each dot?"

"They move. The dots *move*. Actually, as he explained it, they are not dots so much as – smudges of colour. But they shift – blend sometimes, apparently. And the overall shape changes too."

"What on earth does it all mean?"

"Search me. But I tell you, he had me on edge. I didn't know whether I wanted him to keep telling me or to stop. Oh, and he described what his friend's voice is like."

"Which is...?"

"Deep – sort of boomy. He said it seems to come from everywhere, not just the colours. And his friend keeps up with him when he is walking but if Robbie turns and looks right at him he moves away."

"Disappears?"

"No, just goes further away."

Marlene and I puzzled over all this, as you might imagine. We have a friend, an English teacher at the high school, who is by way of being a bit of a psychoanalyst. He remembered Robert very well, and said he had shown good scholastic ability in his early years, "but then he drifted off into his own world." I told him about the new thing.

He said that there would have been a trigger for this and that we could probably discover what it had been. He said it could be something Robert had read, or a story he had heard from someone.

***

Next time I drove Robert out I asked him if he had seen his friend again.

"Yes – yesterday – and you know where?"

"No, where?"

"At Hoffman's."

This is a roadside rest area for motorists about ten kilometres up river.

"What were you doing there?"

"I got a lift on Mister Garvin's log truck. I walked back in the trees."

"And your friend met you up there?"

"Yes. – after a few minutes. He came all the way back with me."

"Did you talk much?"

"Yes, we talked all the time."

"Can you remember what he told you?"

"No", and he looked over to me and gave a smile, an 'I know that is a bit funny' smile.

I have never been much of a hugger of our own son Timmie – not like a lot of people seem to go in for nowadays – but it seemed natural to reach over and give my passenger a squeeze on the neck. I was rewarded with big smile of what seemed to be pure joy.

Three days later and another development. His friend had revealed that he is as much at home in the water as in the forest.

I knew that Robert used to borrow his uncle's dinghy, which was tied up at a jetty near their home. He had told me some of the places he had reached by rowing and they were surprisingly far. It was no wonder the lad had such well developed shoulders, and was so strong.

This day he had gone up to Bergin's Landing, which is a good hour's row, and had just decided to turn about when his friend joined him.

"I could see him in the water. Just near me."

"What does he look like in the water?"

"The same colour as the water," with a hint of 'of course'. And I now got a lecture on the colours of water – causing me to reflect again about his high powers of observation of things natural – really much more acute than mine.

"But if he is the same colour as the water Robert, how could you see him?"

This time I got an almost pitying look. "Of course I could see him!"

I had a thought. "When we get to our place will you do a drawing for Marlene like you did before?"

"Yes."

That effort though must have taxed him. Marlene told me he screwed up several pieces of paper before he was more or less satisfied. While he was off at the dairy again my wife and I studied the result.

He had 'got' the water by placing one layer of colour over the other – the colours that he told me he saw in our river – blue and green and brown – but that was all *we* could see. Or all *I* could see anyhow. I looked blankly at Marlene but she said "I can see it – him" and she turned the paper around for me and yes, I could see, from the new angle, a sort of shape – but I can't for the life of me describe what I was looking at.

***

Three days later and Robert told us his friend had joined him the previous day when he was again out in the dinghy. He told us his friend played tricks on him, being first on one side of the boat and then the other.

"Sometimes he goes a long while underneath me."

"How do you know he's there?"

"Because he talks to me."

"Under the water!?"

"Oh yes. He talks with me wherever we are."

"I wonder why he spends so much time with you?"

"Because I'm his friend!"

"Do you think he has any other friends?" I asked, but Marlene touched my foot under the table; I took that to mean she thought I might have been going too far. Perhaps I was, because the boy grew silent after that, and went off to play with my two dogs.

***

A few days after this, at the Jansen's, while Robert was at the ute patting my dogs – they are besotted with him – I asked Else if she knew about this new friend. Yes, he had told her. I asked her what she made of it.

"Well – I'm used to the – unreality."

"But it's so real to *him*!"

"Well he has marvellous imagination, wouldn't you say?"

"I would, but – this is more than imagination."

"Yes it is." She looked at me seriously. "When he was little – before any of this showed up – he had an Aboriginal friend. They used to spend all their time together. Every weekend they'd go off all day into the bush, up and down the river."

I was excited by this. Was I getting closer to something?

"The boy had an uncle – well, an older relative, you know how they have all these "uncles" – he was living with the family for a time. Robert used to come back here with all these stories. Aboriginal stories. Some of them were about the creatures that live in the bush here. Their heads were absolutely filled. I didn't worry about it. Well you know I am Scottish, and we don't mind a bit of legend and monster madness. Fey and all that."

"The Bunyip!" She nodded. "The books say 'never clearly seen', and ' a booming voice'...Oh Elsie, that's what it is. *He's remembered a story.*"

As I was getting into the ute she said " you know, many white settlers in the early days believed in the Bunyip too."

As soon as I got home I told Marlene about the conversation – my discovery.

"Of course!" Marlene leaned back in her chair. "When I was growing up old-timers used to talk about it. *They* certainly seemed to believe in it. In the forest *and in the water too*. The lagoons more than the river though."

"Did anyone ever say they had *seen* it?"

"I don't think so. But people did say they heard that booming sound..."

About a month after that Robert told us that his friend was now visiting him at the *house,* coming into his room at night.

"I always sleep with my windows open. I can tell when he comes because the curtains move. They are very heavy and they come right down to the floor, but they move", and he swayed. "He comes every night but he doesn't stay long. I wake up and see the curtains move and he's there. I've asked him why he has come but he hasn't told me."

I told him that his uncle and aunt would like to know this.

"But this is my friend."

"They are your friends too. Friends tell each other things. Like you and me."

***

Two mornings later Elsie rang.

"Gerry's getting someone to come and do another assessment on Robert."

"Is something wrong?" She had sounded tense.

"Robert pushed Gerry over. Really hard."

"Why? Did Gerry do something?"

"Yes. Well all he did was try to close Robert's window. It was really cold this morning in here."

"But Robert believes..."

"I know – but Gerry – anyhow the man is coming later this afternoon."

***

Robert walked out early the following morning. He sat at our kitchen table, looking unhappy.

"A man wants me to go with him to Albury."

"When?"

"Tomorrow."

***

When I ran Robert back to town in the late afternoon I saw Elsie.

"It's to do some tests. But Gerry is thinking Robert might be better in some sort of Home. He says he might hurt one of us."

"He would never do that."

"That's what I think. But Gerry's worried. About me probably."

***

I was on edge all the next day, and in the evening I rang.

" They're not back. They're staying there tonight." She paused. "He punched someone Frank. *Two* people."

"Who? Why?"

"They took him to see one of those community houses they have. He must have thought they were trying to make him stay there. There was a big struggle apparently. They – they had to sedate him." And she started to cry. "I should have gone with them."

"Is there something you would like us to do? Would it be a good idea if Robert came and stayed here for a while?"

"Oh yes, that would be terrific. We'll – we'll see."

***

The following night I rang again.

160

"Yes he's back. For now. But Gerry's mind is made up. He'll have to go – somewhere."

"We'll take him." I said, just like that.

***

So now, breakfast time the next morning, and I'm working up to telling – asking – Marlene. I think she'll probably say no. And even if she doesn't she will have big doubts. If Robert has pushed Gerry and punched a couple of men – would she and I always be safe? And then there are our granddaughters – and even our share farmers, Roger and Sue.

I go to the fridge to get out the marmalade. As I close the door I look again at Robert's drawings which Marlene has stuck there. She notices me looking at them.

"Do you remember that song. 'There was a boy – a very strange enchanted boy'? That's our Robert." She walked to the fridge and touched the drawings. "I didn't tell you... after he did this one of his friend in the water he gave me a big hug."

I take a breath – time to speak – but she hasn't finished.

"I've been thinking. We don't use Timmie's room now..."

FOURTEEN

NOTHING WASTED

A horn blew and Vince looked up from scratching the animal's back and waved to his neighbours going past in their station wagon. Tom and Liz must think I live with these pigs, he thought – but he really only came up to them from the house twice a day – perhaps three times.

But seeing his neighbours reminded him that the Silvagnis had said that they would call later in the afternoon, and he needed to grind up some coffee beans beforehand. He stepped over the low fence of the pigs' enclosure and hurried back to the house.

***

He wondered from time to time why people thought he must be lonely – "living out there, on your own... "

Out there? Just along the river, fifteen kilometres from town – less than ten minutes drive? And *lonely?* With a member of the family coming out every few days, and, since Rosa had died, friends and neighbours dropping in at all hours; he couldn't turn around without bumping into someone.

His two nieces seemed to love the place, and their kids certainly did – they couldn't stay away. Then there were his sisters, who often brought a couple of their grandchildren.

Since Rosa's death five years before his life seemed to have filled up with women. Even amongst his neighbours it was mostly the wives that called in, often with a cake or a tuna bake or a lasagna; "I made a bit too much Vince" they would say, maybe to avoid embarrassing him – perhaps themselves too – but he appreciated their kindness.

His brother Tony and his wife came out for Sunday lunch at least once a month. And he knew he could always drop in at any time at their farm, next to the one he and Rosa had owned. No, he was never lonely – his life was crowded with family and friends.

Another thing people said was – "it's dangerous – with the machinery Vince – and all those animals. If you got hurt, how would anyone know?"

What machinery – he didn't have any; it wasn't a farm, it was just ten hectares, – what did they call it these days – a lifestyle block. And *all those animals?* Three cows, five pigs, some chooks and two dogs – how could *they* hurt him? The most he might get from one of his docile cows was a flick from a tail. His hens might peck his hand when he was trying to take eggs from under them – which one in particular now did very determinedly, but she had become his favourite. And his pigs – well they loved him, and he might say that he loved them too – as he loved all his animals.

There were his birds too, which he visited at least twice a day – though he had put big feeders and drinkers in their aviaries so that they could actually last for weeks without his having to add anything – but he liked to look at them. The sulphur crested and the galah still had only small tins, so he had to top them up daily, but that was good because he talked to them. Wally the white one could talk quite a bit himself. He believed that Sulphurs were close to being the smartest of all birds.

He had wallabies too, grazing the lawns right up to his house, and scarcely bothering to hop away if he walked amongst them. They had been wary of his cattle dogs in the beginning but he had taught Bella and Rocco to tolerate them. And although he did not feed the wallabies, he was sure that if he began to do so – some bread perhaps – they would soon be eating from his hand.

Of all his animals though, domesticated or wild, he had to say it was the pigs that were his favourites. He spoilt them, Rosa used to say, but, as he had told her, you *should* spoil pigs because they were the most *productive* of all animals. Pigs repaid you for every morsel of food you gave them – that was why all their farmer friends had some.

Although he had kept pigs for years however, he had never been able to bring himself to kill any. His friend Joe always did that for him, taking them away one day and returning the next with them dressed, ready for Vince to cut up.

***

After it had become clear that neither of their boys wanted to go on with their fruit orchard it had made sense to sell out to his brother Tony next door. He and Rosa had hoped to stay on in their farmhouse but Tony's Angelo had got engaged and they could see he would need it.

They had just about made up their mind to buy a house in town when someone showed them the ad for the farmlet – not irrigated like their orchard but with the right to take some water from the channel for house and garden and livestock.

Rosa had started a big garden and he'd put the back eight hectares under pasture, bought three Jersey cows – having in mind getting young calves from time to time for them to rear – and bought a handful of weaner pigs from one of their new neighbours.

He had marked out a half-hectare enclosure for the pigs next to the garden. Rosa was agreeable to his keeping pigs but not, she insisted, so close to the house; she did not want the smell. He had obliged her by moving their run a further hundred metres away; he put in an automatic drinker and a grain feeder that would hold a week's supply, and half an old water tank, upside down, for shelter. From then it had become his greatest pleasure to pull on his "pig boots" – a pair of old joggers – and take the short walk up to see them.

He could always see them waiting for him at the fence; how did they know he was coming? Did they hear him? Perhaps they smelt him; he could always smell *them* from a distance. It was funny how Rosa had objected to the smell; it was strong yes, but not, he thought, *bad*. Once you knew what a smell was, well – you accepted it. He did anyhow.

Rosa had hardly ever visited his friends – and would laugh at his dedication to them; "you treat them like royalty." Yes, well, that paid off; well fed and contented pigs gave the best meat.

They always greeted him with grunts and snuffles. He would step over the low barrier and scratch their ears and their backs. They would seek his hands for the delights he brought – some over-ripe fruit, or pieces of bread.

They would in fact eat *anything* he brought – a rotted cabbage, some potatoes – *anything*. And things he did *not* bring them. One of the laying hens, who were free to range everywhere, had died in the top end of their enclosure; two days later there was nothing left but a few feathers. Rosa had reckoned they would eat *him* one day.

He thought that they would do a thorough job of that too. He recalled times when he and his brother had hunted wild ones in the timbered country further along the river, and they had come upon the remains of a cow or bull. There was very little left – just the horns, and a few of the very thickest of the bones – always scattered widely; a week after an animal had died it was almost impossible to tell where its carcass would have originally lain.

After he had given the pigs their treats he would walk around the perimeter of their half-hectare enclosure, the animals trotting along beside and behind him. Neighbours going along the nearby road would see him and toot.

And every few months, when a couple had reached the right size and condition, he would call up Joe. When his friend had brought the carcases back the next day he would bone them out, for the pancetta, the prosciutto, the sosoguce, the capocollo and of course the salami. He enjoyed the process – the cutting, and the rubbing in of the salt and the herbs and spices.

All the family came out on these days, to help with the preparations, and to enjoy a rib barbecue. Sometimes his two boys would come up from the city, bringing girlfriends.

These were very happy occasions for Vince – the adults drinking some of Tony's wine, the little ones running about – in summer on the vine-shaded verandahs, in winter out on the lawn. Before they left – the last thing – the family would help him string up the salami in loops under the garage roof.

After everyone had gone he would walk around and inspect his handiwork, the meats that were now beginning to cure. He would take a pride in the fact that every gram had been used. He might say that he had *honoured* his friends: nothing had been wasted.

***

At the end of this particular family day, he walked up to the enclosure. They were at the fence as usual, grunting in pleasure and anticipation. Only three now – he would have to go to Frank's during the week and get another couple of weaners. He stepped over the fence and began handing out some of the peaches Tony had brought.

No neighbours' vehicles went past this day; his road had been very quiet for the previous week. He knew that everyone was busy trying to make hay; there had been rain, and it had made the work difficult. He thought he probably wouldn't get any visits for a while.

When each of the pigs had had its treat Vince walked across to look in the grainfeeder. Lower than he thought – just enough for one day; he would need to bring up a couple of bags in his wheelbarrow tomorrow. They were eating well; it was a good sign when animals were right onto their food.

He turned to step off the concrete apron on which the feeder rested. One of his friends was standing very close and Vince lifted his leg to step across him. The pig moved away at the same moment and Vince lost his balance. He fell, landing hard, and his head whipped back and struck the edge of the concrete apron.

***

His sister in law drove out with one of her daughters the following day to collect some of the meat Vince had promised them. In the house yard they called out for him but got no response. The younger woman went to the back garden gate and looked down the paddock to where she could see the three cows standing in the shade of the gum tree in the far corner. She told her mother she thought she could see her uncle there with them. They knew which of the pieces they were to take and they were in a hurry so they collected them and drove away.

No other member of the family came out during the rest of the week, which was normal following a special family pig weekend, but no-one came out the next weekend either. One of Vince's daughters rang on the Saturday but when there was no reply she left a "hello" message, and said not to bother ringing back – she would come out mid-week. .

None of the neighbours dropped by either, busy with their hay-making.His daughter left another message mid week; two of the children had bad colds and she would not be out.

It was not until the Saturday, two weeks after the family pig day, that the first visitors arrived – his brother Tony and wife Estelle and one of their daughters.

As they got out of the car the daughter said "something's wrong'; no barking had greeted them, and when the two dogs did appear, instead of running in welcome they approached at a walk They were hollow sided and their eyes were sunken.

The older woman rushed into the house, running first to her brother-in-law's bedroom then the bathroom and then right through the house. "He's not here!" she yelled to the others and the trio began a fevered search of the garden and sheds. As they went around they noticed that the white cockatoo and the galah were dead, though the smaller birds – the finches and the budgerigars – were still alive.

Tony and the daughter drove the station wagon out through the back gate of the garden, heading to where they could see the three cows under the gum tree. Estelle went up to the pigs.

***

She had never been to the enclosure before; she found the pigs waiting for her at the fence. They too were hollow sided but seemed to be in a stronger condition than the dogs.

She could see across the whole enclosure from where she stood but she knew she had to do a thorough job and walk right around it; Vince was not there. She heard her husband's vehicle returning – perhaps they had found him she thought – and it would be his body probably, she told herself – that was the likely thing.

She was about to step across the fence when – a farmer's wife – she thought to check the feeder. Empty – the pigs needed feed. .

Now she did step over the fence and began to hurry back towards the house. If the others had not found him she would have nothing to add. She had seen only the pigs, their shelter, the water trough and the empty feed bin. Nothing else – a few bones and – near the fence – an old jogger.

FIFTEEN

THE WAITRESS

Our youngest boy is very dexterous. He knows it, and shows off sometimes.

If, at breakfast, the milk jug has not yet been put on the table but is still on the bench behind him, he will reach back, grasp the handle and, swinging the jug around fast, will bring it to a halt above the middle of the table. He does this without spilling a drop or, seemingly, without even causing the milk to slop within the jug. He then pours it into cup or glass.

Guests gasp, Damian smirks and family members groan. I look over at Jenny and get a particular smile.

***

I should have been back at my office to complete a report for my partners but I was continuing to sit in the café drinking coffee. I had made some notes on a napkin—telling myself I was working—but it was something else that was keeping me. Or someone.

She was old for a regular waitress, I mean *older*, perhaps mid thirties. Trim figure. Lots of wavy hair, a rich chestnut. Her face was the clincher though – intelligent and good humoured; it was a strong face that lit up when she smiled.

She was walking towards me now, coffee carafe in hand; I thought she looked tired. As she neared she raised her eyebrows and I nodded. While she was pouring I suggested she take a break and a little to my surprise she pulled out the chair opposite and sat.

"Well, it's nearly over."

The café was new – just a fortnight old; it was small but nicely situated, just on the edge of our town's business area and right next to the river. I thought that the owners could do well; I had twice taken clients there for lunch.

At this moment there were only two other tables occupied, a young couple at one and three men at a table near me. The men were discussing a real estate deal. One of them was a big burly bloke with a loud voice.

"I thought you looked tired."

She looked at me a moment. "You've been in here a couple of times."

"Yes. We have an office around the corner. The architects..."

She nodded. "I park in your customer space at the back sometimes. If I'm late."

"Anytime..."

"Thanks." That nice smile again, and then "yes I am tired. Worried more." A pause. "My boy..."

I took a guess "Sole custody...?"

"You're sharp. Yeah."

I pointed to my chest."Three boys."

She slowly sat back and looked at me; I had her full interest.

"How old?"

"Nineteen, seventeen and fifteen."

"Damian's twelve. He used to be – lovely." Her voice trailed off, then "he wanted to meet some of his mates last night down at that game room but I didn't like the sound of it." She shrugged. "I got called some names."

On impulse I reached across and gave her arm a pat. "It passes. He'll come good."

She was about to say something when there was a call from the men's table.

"Can we have some more coffee?"

"Excuse me" she said, and walked to their table. Only the man with the loud voice wanted a cup. The young couple at the other table stood up and she went with them to the cash register.

Then – "this is bloody cold!" Shouted.

"Sorry sir" she called, "I'll bring you another."

"You'd better" he said. I thought his companions looked embarrassed.

She walked down to the coffee bar at the rear. I watched her as she checked the temperature of the second carafe. She seemed calm, unflustered by the man's manner.

The man held his cup out at arm's length. "It's better if you put it on the table sir."

"No, do it there."

She began to pour but stopped. " No, really sir, please put it down. You're moving."

"I'm bloody well not."

I watched her face. *I* was getting angry but there was no obvious reaction from her.

This time the coffee went onto the sleeve of his suit.

"Bloody hell!" and he shot to his feet. His chair fell over and his cup went flying; the other two quickly pushed themselves back from the table.

The man began tearing off his jacket, dancing with rage. His leg caught one of the legs of the overturned chair and he fell backwards. "Christ!" he bellowed. The other two looked at each other and, I thought, exchanged smiles.

When order was restored the woman offered to take the coat and sponge it.

"Don't bother."

"Would you still like another coffee sir?"

One of the other men stifled a laugh and Burly glared at him.

"What I'd like is the manager."

"I'm the manager sir."

"Well the owner then."

"That's me."

"Bloody hell! Yes I *would* like another coffee. In my *cup.*"

This time the man left the cup on the table while she poured. As she walked towards me she looked down and gave a little grin; she no longer looked tired. She had however just passed me when there was another bellow.

"I want milk. Where's the bloody milk? Jesus Christ!"

When she went back I noticed she was carrying not one of those little café jugs but a wide mouthed two litre glass jug, and it was full. Something told me to keep watching.

As she reached the table she stumbled, as if she had caught her heel in the carpet. The entire two litres of milk left the jug in a beautiful curve and landed down the front of the man, saturating him from neck to lap.

The bellow this time was deafening. He shot to his feet and again his chair fell and again he tripped over its legs. The other two, far from going to his aid, exploded into laughter. Burly thrashed around on the floor, his efforts to regain his feet hampered by chair legs, and the others lost it completely, standing and holding onto each other, rocking backwards and forwards. I thought that they too could soon end up on the floor.

When Burly eventually got to his feet, all red face and bulging eyes, milk dripping from shirt and tie, the men looked at him in what I thought was an attempt to show some concern but they were set off again. The waitress had retired to a serving bench and was leaning against it, shaking with laughter.

It was just classic: oh for a camera. And there was more. Burly righted his chair and slumped down heavily onto it; it collapsed. This set us all off again – me too, you can imagine. I don't know if a group of people has ever laughed as long or as loudly – in the history of the world.

***

Her boy gets along terrifically with my three; perhaps it was all meant to be. Jenny and I have doubled the size of the café and I spend a lot of my spare time there. I even do some of the waiting. Jenny has agreed that if our friend comes in again I shall be the one to serve him. To my regret it hasn't yet happened.

SIXTEEN

SOUNDS AT DAD'S

"I heard a new sound Grandad."

Jessica is six and is just back with her eight year old brother from a visit to *my* father's place. They call him Grandpa.

"It went 'mmmmmm'." She is dissatisfied with her effort and tries again, this time frowning first, dropping her chin and trying to deepen her voice. "Mmmmmm."

"Like a cow does when she starts a moo?"

"Yes, but it was very quiet."

"Do you know what it was?"

"No. I didn't see."

Her brother Jeremy says "I heard a peewit" and I think, this'll be interesting. He gathers himself and takes a breath but nothing comes. He looks puzzled.

"Peewits are very hard" I say. "I don't think *I* can do it."

I give it a go, and produce something that is between a whistle and a squawk and we all laugh.

"How about we make some pikelets?"

***

I raised their mother, my daughter Christine, in this town on the Murray River. I was raised here myself, but on my father's small irrigation fruit farm, which is right on the edge of town. I worked on it with Dad until we decided ten years ago to sell it. We kept an acre with the old homestead, and the old man has continued to live on there. Lately I have tried to persuade him to move, into something smaller and more modern here in town, but he prefers to stay. I must say though that he manages very well, cooking for himself and keeping quite a large vegetable garden.

***

Christine went to Melbourne, for uni and then a job, and then found herself a very nice partner in Mark. They were living in a flat in Carlton when they started a family, and they decided to continue the urban life. They purchased a larger apartment in a new development in Albert Park.

It was during one of their visits up here about three years ago that I first noticed that things that were everyday to me struck the littlees as novelties, especially things at Grandpa's. Like the boot scraper at the back door, the tall mantel clock with its long pendulum, and the slow combustion stove; they were fascinated when we opened the little door in the front of the stove and put in another piece of wood. And their space age jug at home certainly did not send up a column of steam like Grandpa's big black kettle. They had never seen someone make *a pot of tea*.

On a visit I made to Melbourne a little later I met Jeremy's teacher when I walked to the school to pick him up. She said the boy had been full of talk about what he had seen at his Grandpa's place and in particular had been keen to repeat for the class the *sounds* – the hiss of the kettle, the crackle of the fire, and the tick-tock of the big clock.

***

Dad's rooster Wally is a Black Leghorn. He is machismo personified, and a great crower, not just at dawn but at any time of the day, from sunup to sundown. Of course you cannot keep a rooster in a town area these days, or perhaps you can if you somehow prevent it from crowing, but because Dad is on the edge of town, and at least four hundred metres from the nearest dwelling, he gets away with it. It is just as well he is so removed because Wally's call *carries*; it is a ringing challenge to roosters up and down the river.

I happened to be with young Jeremy in Dad's kitchen the first time he heard Wally. I can remember his head jerking up, and his blue eyes widening in wonder. We hurried outside, to find Wally perched on the post beside the garden tap – his favourite crowing position – and I knew we were in for a recital. Another rooster, a long way off – it must have been at another farmhouse – replied to Wally's challenge, and it was on. It was fun to watch Jeremy while Wally performed – he was enthralled. I too found myself looking afresh at the bird, the way he thrust out his chest and raised himself to full height – on tiptoes as it were – and flapped his wings before each call, as if that helped him fill his lungs with air.

That evening back at my house Jeremy told the rest of his family about Wal. I do a fair representation of a rooster's crow and let a couple go. Jeremy's eyes shone; Jessica demanded to be taken out the next day to see and hear for herself.

Wally did entertain Jessica and then so did a magpie. Dad has always fed maggies, just outside the back door, though I have known some of those cheeky birds to actually come right into his kitchen. Jess and I were throwing pieces of mutton fat onto the path when one of the birds lifted its head and began carolling. The bird did this even though it had a fairly substantial piece of fat in its mouth. I had seen them do this before; it's a remarkable feat – and they can keep it up for several minutes.

Jess was delighted. That evening she had her own story to tell – and I had to do another imitation.

***

Now, as soon as the family arrives at my place, I am put under great pressure by the children to take them straight out to Grandpa's. And for some reason I cannot quite fathom, it is the *sounds* rather than the sights that delight them.

What sounds? Well – take a *hen*. There's that low continuous sound she produces as she goes scratching and foraging about; Jessica says she is *talking*. Then there is the urgent "duk duk duk" to her chicks when she has found something for them to eat – the loud repeated squawk when she has just laid – the strange whirring sound when she spies a hawk overhead (and how quickly does she spot it, even when it is at a considerable height), and then there is that loud call of alarm or excitement when something has disturbed her. You can hear all of those sounds in a day at Dad's.

It was Jeremy who first made me aware of *the hum of bees* when they are working blossom. Dad has a bottlebrush just outside his bedroom window and when in flower it drips with nectar. We were standing near it when Jeremy held up a finger; I have come to learn that this means whoa – listen – what's that? At first I couldn't make out what had taken his attention. I suppose I could hear the bees right enough but I wasn't thinking that it was a sound that should be *listened to* – and in his case, identified.

Because it was safe – the bees totally absorbed in gathering nectar – I took him up very close to a brush and we watched the bees. In Melbourne apparently the kids had never seen or perhaps more accurately noticed bees, and certainly never listened to them.

***

Dad keeps the big black kettle at the back of the stove as a reservoir; it is rarely brought to the boil. When he does want to boil water he decants some into a smaller aluminium flat bottomed kettle. This one has a whistle, and its sound is piercing. The first time the two heard it they were almost frightened.

They swore they had never heard a *postman's* whistle either until they were out there. Though Dad is strictly speaking outside the town's mail delivery area the local postman takes his bike up those extra few hundred metres of road. And though he doesn't routinely blow his whistle any more he does do it for Dad.

Because Dad is surrounded by paddocks that have livestock, the children can hear cattle lowing and sheep bleating. And crows of course – and those birds do make a wonderful variety of sounds, from "ark ark" to chortles and even whistles – and there are the screeches of the sulphur cresteds and the galahs and the corellas, and the calls and songs of the finches and wrens, butchers, whistlers and wagtails. Our two particularly love crested pigeons – that whirring hum during display, and the whistle of their wings when they take off.

Our visits together have made *me* more attuned to the sounds at Dad's, like that of rain on the old roof, and the creaking of that same iron on a hot day as it heats up, the scratchy ring of the old front door bell, the carrying note produced by a wooden spoon on a ceramic mixing bowl and the rattle of an old eggbeater. And when Dad is out in his shed in the garden, the ring of metal on metal.

***

The two are having fun dropping spoonfuls of batter onto the griddle.

Later in the afternoon they and their mother intend to go out again to my father's. This morning they had found no – one at home, but the back door open. Christine said she assumed a neighbour had dropped by and they had taken off somewhere.

The two eat the pikelets as fast as I can turn them out. Jessica repeats for us the strange sound she heard in the garden.

"Mmmmmm."

"Whereabouts?"

"Near the shed."

"*Under* it ?"

"No."

"Did you look inside the shed?"

"No. I couldn't push the door open."

That is odd. The door doesn't have a catch. I get up and ring my father but there is no answer. I call Christine and we get in the car; Mark stays with the children.

At Dad's we go to the shed and I try to open the door. There is something heavy leaning against the door. I look in at the small side window and see my father lying on the floor, his head and shoulders against the door. I call out and see his hand move.

With Christine watching from the window I push slowly against the door. She tells me I am rolling my father onto his stomach. When I have enough room I slide in through the gap. Dad can hear me but does not seem to be able to speak. He grabs my arm though, and with surprising strength. Chris calls the ambulance.

***

It was some kind of turn. Not a heart attack the doctors tell us, and not a stroke either. They find that his blood pressure is low, and prescribe stuff. He should recover quickly they say, and be back home within days – more or less back to normal.

"Sound", you might say.

SEVENTEEN

THE VISIT

I have just put my visitor on his plane; he should be back in Melbourne in a couple of hours. He'll need some help there though, to get home – even to get out of the plane. It was quite a job getting him *in*.

My old school friend shook my hand at the end, even thanking me for the hospitality, which I thought was gracious. Considering.

***

Nige and I were not *mates* at school. For one thing I was a Boarder and he was a 'Day', so we just didn't spend that much time together. That wasn't the main reason we weren't buddies though.

He was a 'good' kid see and I was probably thought of as *not*. There was no way I was 'bad', let me say. I've always been rather drawn to that expression 'high-spirited'; I could also go along with 'fun – loving'.

At home here on "Urangee" I was allowed to do doughnuts in our old ute on the flat in front of the homestead. I used to climb trees, though my mother *was* twitchy about that, and I swam in the dams

– even waterskied on them with my mates, behind said ute, which was a bit tricky.

At Boarding School when there's not much doing on a weekend you really have to make your own fun. So, yes, some of us would go over the swimming pool fence on hot nights – and if there was an interesting looking bird's nest in one our elms we went up to have a look. And what better place to try out a mate's car than in the big visitor's parking area? Late at night of course, when there was no-one else around. We thought.

I think that even if Nige had been a Boarder he still wouldn't have done things like that. He was a good batsman though, and I was more than useful in that department, so we were both in the same cricket team – eventually the "A". That's how we got to know each other a bit.

Nige did very well in his exams and went on to Uni and did Law. And I feel I can say that *I* would have done well too, if I had studied. Example: without any work at all I always came near the top of my Year in English; I always did have a bit of a way with words. Mr. Pacey my English teacher wanted me to do Arts and go into journalism or something like that.

But – Dad had heart trouble and needed me on the place, and I was brought back home in the middle of my last year. He and Mum by the way were getting on a bit when they had me, (and obviously decided that one was enough).

"Urangee" is right in the middle of the Riverina plain, about two hours drive north of the Murray River. I have to say I loved coming back – and I still love it here.

Still single too – though I've come dangerously close to the big M a couple of times. My present girlfriend reckons I'm not ready – "not mature enough' was, if I remember, her unnecessarily harsh way of putting it.

We have a good social life out here though. Visitors think because there aren't many people around and it's a long way to our nearest town – and that *is* pretty small – that there's no 'life' here. They're wrong – there's all the sport you can handle, and we're always having barbecues and parties and dances and even balls.

There *are* times when I am out in one of our big back paddocks, and I've switched off the ute's engine or killed the bike – and it's very quiet – that I do feel the remoteness. The silence – or perhaps just the sound of a light breeze in a tree – or a bird calling – that's when it hits me. But it's a good hit.

I know this – space – can freak some people, especially city ones like Nige. Though I think *he* actually liked it – or would have.

***

He rang me up from Melbourne last week, out of the blue; one of his colleagues in the law firm had a pilot's licence and was flying up to the Murray for the weekend, for a wedding. Nige could get a lift; could I drive in to the airstrip and take him back to my place for the weekend?

"You told me so much about the place Bunny (my school nickname: real name Bernard). I'd love to see what its like."

No worries. Well, *one* worry – a small one. As a twenty six year old bachelor with no parents around – Mum and Dad live in on the River now – my housekeeping in the old homestead leaves a bit to be desired. Apparently.

A whirlwind clean up was called for – but the way I see it, that's one of the values of visitors. I vacuumed the floors, cleaned out the more evil looking things from the fridge, and put clean sheets on a bed.

If I may say so myself, the odd visitor has a good night here – I think I'm a thoughtful host – plenty of beer – or whisky or wine – a comfortable night's sleep and plenty of good food; no-one's ever got food poisoning.

***

Blue Heelers are great dogs – hard working and loyal – especially loyal. Great guard dogs too; if I left Knuckles in the back of the ute in Collins Street with a million dollars just sitting there loose I know it would all be there when I returned. Even *Lygon Street*. Knuckles has this intent way of looking at strangers that seems to unnerve them, and his growl comes straight from hell. He never has to bite. Almost never.

Knuck didn't growl at Nige but as my visitor went to put his bag in the back of the ute he received *the look*. Nige froze. I laughed – it always amuses me how my dog freaks people. (My girlfriends have sometimes said unnecessarily harsh things about that too).

I stood beside Nige while he lowered the bag . Knuck watched the bag all the way down, looking, you'd have to say, deeply suspicious.

I ruffled my old friend's neck – the dog's not the man's – and tried to persuade him to come closer and give Nige's hand a lick – Knuck is a great licker – but he seemed to think that was taking things too far, and stayed in the middle of the ute.

I did think it was a bit unfriendly of Knuckles, but then he *can* be like that. Occasionally. With some people.

We dropped in and said hello to Mum and Dad – Nige had met them once when they came down to Melbourne – and we were on our way out of town again by ten o'clock. I gabbed on about things – doing the tour guide thing; Nige didn't say much – didn't ask as many questions as I thought he might.

I noticed he was looking left and right a lot, even turning and looking back through the rear window. Eventually he said "there's nothing here is there?"

Well, you do get that – with city visitors. They just see a flat plain – no animals – no houses – no people.

I see lots of things – a few sheep grazing in a dry creek – some galahs on a fence – the dust from a vehicle – an eagle building a nest in a tree – a windmill working flat out – a little mob of crows, which tells me there's probably a dead animal nearby – a patch of green grass that means a leak in a pipeline; they're all little stories – but urban visitors can't read them.

Anyhow, when we pulled up at the homestead that did impress my visitor. The house is old and very big, and there is a humungous garden and lots of sheds; people say my home is more like a *settlement*. I told Nige to leave his bag and we'd walk around it all to get him orientated.

That took more than half an hour – Nige had a lot of questions now, mainly about the history – and then I went in to get some lunch ready while he went back to get his bag. Bad move.

Although I was in the kitchen, which is right at the back of the house, I heard the shout. I rushed out; Nige was standing some two metres from the side of the ute, holding his arm, and Knuckles, with his head over the side of the ute, was looking intently at him. It was that look again.

"He bit me!"

"What did you do?"

"What did *I* do? Nothing!"

"You must have..." I stopped myself. Wrong thing to say. I hurried forward, genuinely concerned, and inspected Nige's forearm. No blood, no broken skin, just a ring of teethmarks. So Knuckles hadn't really *bitten* him; if he had there would have been a lot more damage.

"That's not really..." but I stopped myself again; I *am* learning that it is sometimes best not to say just whatever is in one's mind. "We'll wash it and I'll put a bandage on it if you want. Probably get a bruise there." *Definitely* get a bruise there; Knuck has jaws that can crack cow bones.

I turned and lifted Nige's bag out and ruffled Knuckles ears.

"Aren't you going to say something to the dog!?"

Tricky. Knuckles had really only been *doing his job*. "Look, I'm sorry Nige, but – it's hard to explain – dogs are territorial, and when he is in the ute that's his territory too. It was my fault. I should have got you to spend longer with him before."

As we walked to the house I got the feeling that as an excuse Nige thought this somewhat lacked, so I added "he'll be right with you now, I promise.", but actually I wasn't too sure. Knuckles is getting a bit difficult with people. Some people.

Maybe, I thought, Nige had *frightened* the dog – but then that's ridiculous; nothing frightens him. Perhaps Nige had shown that *he* was frightened – that wouldn't have helped. I didn't say any more – best to move on, as they say. I would try and get the two palled up.

After lunch – corned beef and pickle sandwiches, and a beer – I did just that, with Nige throwing a ball and Knuck retrieving it. I showed my visitor that he could even take the ball directly out of the dog's mouth, though I warned him not to try to do that with anything that he *hadn't* thrown. And, while we were on the general subject – and not that Nige would ever have done it – I warned him against attempting to wrestle with me while Knuckles was around. This dog is nothing if not loyal.

***

We took off on a tour of the place on the bikes, me on the 250 and him on the 150. Nige said he could handle a bike because he used to go into the uni on one. I took him out onto the flat, especially where there was a bit of rough going, so he could get the feel of it – cross country is a lot different to a smooth city road. He did get the wobbles to begin with but after a while seemed to be okay so off we went. I didn't go fast, and to start off we were on our own graded tracks anyhow.

We went right out to the back of the place, which took us half an hour. Every now and then I would pull up and I'd tell him about things – the sheep and the trees and the grasses – me in full verbal flight – and he seemed quite interested. He said it was all great; when I asked about his arm he said it was sore but wasn't bothering him.

I was taking the opportunity to check the water troughs as well, cruising up alongside each one to see if its float was working properly. About half way back to the house and coming up alongside one trough – Nige about fifty metres behind me – I saw a big Brown, about five metres out and coming in. They do this to get a drink – most troughs have a drip somewhere. I accelerated ahead about ten metres, spun around and put up my hand; the snake and Nige could be arriving at the trough together.

Nige looked at me and pulled a questioning face but *kept coming*. I put both hands up and pumped out a vehement stop signal. He slowed but still came on.

Nige stopped at last but *right beside the snake*. He turned off the engine and said "what?"

"Snake snake!" I shouted, probably a bit hysterically, and pointed at the ground beside him. By now the snake was taking an interest in matters, and had reared up. Nige looked.

They talk about people doing something 'in one bound'. My friend now left his bike in a single arcing movement. The bike fell onto the concrete apron beside the trough but Nige landed *in* the trough – which of course was full of water.

I rushed over to help him – watching for the snake, but it had decided that this was all too much and was heading back the way it had come, flat out.

Nige had landed awkwardly, half on his back, and because of the semi-circular shape of the trough he was having difficulty getting out. I'm pretty strong though and he came out with one decent pull. He spluttered a bit and I thought he must have swallowed some water. He had, but that wasn't the main reason he was spluttering.

"What the hell did you make me stop there for?" He was shouting.

"I didn't."

"You did! You put your hands up!" and he gave a vigorous demonstration of my signals.

"I was trying to get you to stop back there!"

"Well – bloody hell – what was I supposed to think?" and did things with his arms again, somehow now making my signals look ridiculous.

It was hard to know what to say. I did say "you're bleeding."

Blood was running down his cheek from up above his hairline. He bent his head and I could see a cut; he must have hit the concrete cover over the float.

He rested a bit on the side of the trough and I offered to go back to the house and get the ute but he said it was alright, he thought he could still handle the bike.

Back in the kitchen I looked at his wound. The skin was split but I didn't think it needed stitching. I snipped the hair from around it and washed it with peroxide. While Nige continued to dab at it with some iodine on cotton gauze I made us a cup of tea. I suggested we have a rum and he immediately agreed. I changed from tea to coffee – rum seems to go better with coffee.

I asked him how his arm was – from the bite.

"Bit sore."

He rolled his sleeve up and when I unwound the bandage we were both impressed by how quickly the arm had coloured up. It had swollen quite a bit too.

The coffee or probably the rum had some effect because my friend, after a bit, gave a laugh and said that he was well and truly initiated now and surely nothing further could happen.

***

I let Nige have some quiet time on the verandah while I did a few chores around the homestead. About four we had another coffee – and I must admit another rum – and I told him I had to pick up some fencing material from one of the paddocks; did he feel up to a drive?

I hitched up the trailer; Nige got into the passenger seat of the ute. Before he could shut the door Knuckles jumped in over his lap and hunkered down between us. I got a lick on the neck and I said "you'll probably..." but that was as far as I got before Nige got one too. He jerked his head away but I told him this was good – Knuckles had accepted him.

At the first gate I suggested to Nige that with his arm and head and all he should leave the gates to me but he insisted that he could manage them. As he got in again he got another big lick from Knuckles.

At the second gate he said that he wouldn't mind travelling on the trailer for a change. I watched in the rear vision mirror as he perched himself on the front of it, and when I saw he was settled, started off again.

We picked up the rolls of netting and the posts. I suggested that if he wanted to get back into the cab we could put Knuck in the trailer – I do look after my guests – but he said no, he was liking the fresh air. "This is what I'm out here for."

He opened the next gate, I drove through and then waited until I could tell from the movement of the trailer that he was back on. I did look in the rear vision mirror to check but all I could see was dog – Knuckles likes to sit close to me.

I moved off, but had gone only a metre or so when I felt a jolt, as if the trailer had run over a log. Bit odd, but it was just the one bump and I felt nothing more so I accelerated away. After a few moments Knuck decided to move over to the passenger window and I casually flicked my eyes at the mirror. *No Nigel.* I braked, and even as I did an awful possibility occurred to me. That jolt.

I got out and looked back. Thank god he was standing. He gave a wave but it was rather a weak one – an 'I'm okay but only just' wave. I ran back.

"You ran over me!"

"Where?' but it was obvious. Across the thighs of his jeans was a wide dusty mark. I couldn't speak.

"I slipped when I was getting on." He was looking at the marks on his jeans as he said this but then he jerked his head up. "Didn't you see I wasn't on?"

"I..." I was going to tell him about the mirror and the dog but decided to let it pass; I didn't think he would be all that interested in any excuse involving Knuckles.

"You should have..." but gave up on that too. "Are you okay?"

"Well, I haven't broken anything I think." That seemed pretty obvious because he was standing with his full weight on his legs. He put his arm over my shoulders and he tried walking.

"How does it feel?"

"How does it feel?" he repeated. His tone was odd – flat – not a tone one often hears. I was reminded of the words I had once read – "his voice was that of a broken man," Though I shouldn't admit it, I had an urge to laugh; I do laugh at inappropriate moments – I have been told – but to my credit I restrained myself. Instead I said "I think you'll have a couple of bruises there."

"Fair dinkum" he said, in that same tone, and *he* gave a short laugh, though not, I thought, with any real humour in it.

I ran a bath for him and he lay in it for a long while. When I called out that I had dinner ready he said he'd like to have it in there. I took it in and almost dropped the tray; you could actually make out the tread marks.

He sat in the kitchen in my dressing gown after that, giving the rum a hiding. By the time he was ready for bed his legs were so stiff he couldn't put his pyjamas on and I had to help. The bruises were beginning to darken.

In the morning he asked me to help him get out of bed. The tyre marks were turning purple, his arm had gone almost black and a thick scab had formed on his cut. All much as one would have expected really.

During breakfast – he said he wasn't very hungry – we got a call from his pilot friend. He'd had a message from Melbourne and he needed to fly back at lunchtime.

Getting Nige into my car was an operation. Eventually we managed, and with the aid of pillows and paracetamol got him more or less comfortable on the back seat; I wondered though how we'd go with the Cessna. I did suggest he should stay for a couple of days before trying to travel – I said I'd be happy to drive him right back to Melbourne – but he seemed determined to leave. The Cessna did prove difficult.

His last words to me were "thanks mate, it's been fun", with another laugh, but you know, this time I think there *was* humour in it. He's got spirit, old Nige.

I'm going to invite him to come up again. For a longer visit. In a while.

EIGHTEEN

THE CARHEW TWIN

Dear Friend and Executor,

I wrote on the front of this envelope "Not to be opened until after you have completed the catalogue" so I am assuming that is done (?) It will look magnificent when printed up, don't you agree? Mine will be the best collection of early Australian furniture ever put to auction.

Almost my first thought after old Doc Ramage delivered the results of those tests was – who can I trust to sell up my stock? You demurred when I first asked you; "I don't know that much about antiques." I think you will have found though that with all my detailed notes and instructions, you have not *needed* to know. And frankly, if I had given the job to one of my antique dealer "friends", there would have been all sorts of deals and underhand shenanigans going on by now. No, you were the one.

This will be a sensational sale – and you will be the "man of the hour!" Enjoy it.

There is just one last thing to ask of you. It will involve you in next to no work – just one small activity in my shop, and one phone call.

Though you might then have to stand back; that phone call will precipitate some swift actions, from others.

If that's a bit mysterious it's appropriate because it *concerns* a mystery, one to which only I have had the key these last years of my life.

***

You asked me one time why Annabelle and I moved our antiques business from Melbourne to your little town on the Murray River; everyone I have had anything to do with has asked me the same question at some time.

What did I tell you – that we wanted a quiet rural life – that we love this river – that the size and geographical position of the town we lived in was not important because we had already established an Australia-wide name – and that this part of the country, being relatively close to Melbourne and our two daughters, gave us the best of both worlds...?

Well, each of those things was true – I did not have to lie to you or anyone there – but I have never told anyone *the single biggest reason* we came here, and that is – Annabelle and I were hunting something. We had been hunting it for *twenty-five years* – and we had come to the conclusion that it was somewhere in this district, and if we were ever to find it we had to settle here.

It was our obsession.

***

I assume you have just taken this letter from the safe and are still in the shop (?) If not, please read no further until you are there, *and at that big secretaire against the back wall,* the only piece in the shop I have not asked you to catalogue – and at which I am writing at this moment.

This piece is not old – it's a reproduction, in your beautiful Red Gum, of a typical Victorian secretaire – glass fronted bookcase above several drawers. When the front of the top drawer is dropped down and gently pulled forward, the desk element emerges, with little compartments and pigeon holes at its rear. It's neat; I have always thought of secretaires as very useful items, and in fact I have used this one up until today, as my office.

But now – are you looking at it? Do you notice anything unusual about it? It *is* a very big example – and made that way for a special reason, but – anything else?

All, as they say, will be revealed. But make yourself comfortable my friend because I have a story to tell you; it is a quite a long one, made even longer because I have added "context" here and there, to help you make full sense of it.

***

The oldest secretaires you find in Australia today were made in England, from oak and walnut and mahogany. Most of the first secretaires that *were* made in this country were also made from these timbers – imported – and generally of mahogany.

There is an existing *Australian* secretaire that was said to be made *in the first decade of the 1800's*. I have been fortunate enough to see it; it is, at least to my eyes, a lovely piece, and very valuable of course. Its value lies in the fact that it was both created early *and from our own timbers* – casuarina and rose mahogany, and some cedar. It was regarded for years by students of Australian furniture as the earliest existing fine piece made from our indigenous timbers – but that was before the *Carhews* were discovered.

***

In 1961 an Australian antiques dealer was holidaying in England. He was going through a 'stately home', as a paying member of the public, when he noticed in one room a pair of secretaires. He knew his timbers and could tell they were of Australian cedar.

He studied them. They were in very good condition, looked to be extremely well made and had fine and unusual detailing. They featured *stringing* – that narrow linear inlay of contrasting timber which craftsmen insert near the edges of doors and drawers, to dress them up, and which in this case terminated at each corner in a nice depiction of what looked like *gum-leaves.*

Each door and drawer handle was elongated, carved into the shape of a *kangaroo lying down.* The very decorative top above the glass doors – what we refer to as a pediment – hosted a carving of a kangaroo and an emu facing each other – a forerunner of our coat of arms.

After the dealer returned to London he found he could not stop thinking about them; *a pair* of secretaires – in *our cedar.* They were probably Australian – made, going by the fauna and flora elements, and the full use of cedar, but *when?* Victorian era Australian – made secretaires are not uncommon but these had *pre*-Victorian characteristics – they looked *Georgian.* (And here my friend a bit more "context" – or *education* if you don't mind. But it's important to the story).

One of the first things a dealer has to learn is to identify styles of antique English furniture. These styles have been given the names of English monarchs. Thus we have William The Fourth, Georgian – early and late (there having been a string of Georges in the eighteenth and early nineteenth centuries) – Victorian, and so on. This aids in dating pieces; of course, styles did not change the very day a monarch died, so there is considerable overlapping.

The person responsible for making this pair of secretaires had made them in a style that we call Georgian – specifically, George the Third. There was the astragal treatment to the glass of the bookcase doors (a hatching of timber, criss-crossing in this case in a diamond pattern, into which the glass had been cut) and the flat, short, slightly splayed feet instead of the turned round ones commonly found on later Victorian era pieces. There was also the narrow raised strip of timber at the very edges of the drawers and doors that we call cock-beading, found also in Victorian furniture but in this case looking to our man somewhat earlier.

These secretaires might well have been made during Victoria's reign, to earlier Georgian design, but the dealer had a hunch that they had actually been made *in the later years of the third George*, who reigned from 1760 to 1820. If they had been made then, that would make them very early Australian pieces indeed, and very valuable.

Our man did what I would have done – he rang the owners of the house. To his immense interest they said they knew the whole story of the pieces – what we call their *provenance* – and invited him to return.

His instincts about the date of manufacture proved to be sound. The owners said the pieces were made in New South Wales in the very first years of British settlement, *possibly even before 1800*, by a convict artisan called Thomas Carhew, on the orders of a settler of some means, Johnathon Beggs. Beggs kept them for a few years and then in 1809 sent them to England as a gift to the Crown. In a letter to the king, which they still had and showed him – it had always been kept in one of the drawers – Beggs wrote that they had been made from a timber " that grows in some abundance here and which is greatly admired for its rich red colour and attractive figuring." It was his hope for the secretaires that "His Majesty might cause them to be displayed in some public building, so that craftsmen and persons of influence could see and appreciate the timber, with the result that a handy export trade might then build up, helping thus to make our colony more self-supporting, and so lighten the burden on the Mother Country."

Well, we know that our timber was *not* taken up – the denser mahogany imported to England from the Caribbean remaining the favoured wood. There is evidence that Australian cedar was thought too soft – 'a bastard mahogany'. Its grain and colour were admired by some, but, by and large, the wood was not widely used, and, if at all, generally only in a secondary way, as lining for things like chests of drawers and wardrobes.

Totally different story out here of course; if one thing characterised the eighteen hundreds in Australia – certainly New South Wales – it was the *use of cedar*; we went mad for it, and not only for furniture; it was used for doors and staircases as well, and, in some houses, whole rooms were panelled in it. Their loss was our gain, in my opinion; it is a lovely wood, soft, yes, but stable, and easy to work, and with that wonderful colour.

***

The Carhew secretaires were placed with a high official in one of the ministries in London and when that man eventually retired, to his grand ancestral home, he took the secretaires with him, evidently now regarding them as his own private property rather than possessions of the Crown.

***

As you can imagine, our twentieth century dealer became very excited. I certainly would have too; I don't think I could have left the country without trying to purchase them. They *pre-dated* the honoured and very valuable specimen I earlier referred to, were in *100 percent cedar*, were a *pair*, had *all provenance*, and with *the maker's initials* on the base. The quinella!

Our man did try to buy them, but the owners were not interested in selling. He asked to be kept informed if the family should ever change its mind, and, again as I would have done, did not leave it at that but 'hassled' them at least once a year.

***

Five years on and the family did decide to sell, informing the dealer in Australia however that they were going to put them up at a Christie's auction. He realised that any chance that he would be able to acquire them at a reasonable figure was gone, and he did the right thing and alerted our National Gallery; at the auction however a private collector from Melbourne outbid the Gallery, and everyone else, paying a new record price. He announced shortly afterwards that he did intend to donate the pair to the National.

When they arrived, the man put them first in his home, a mansion in Toorak. Annabelle and I knew him, and she rang to ask if we could come and see them.

***

As you know my wife and I were partners. She left all the business side to me – the wheeling and dealing – but she was the *scholar*, the real student of the two of us. In fact it was her knowledge of Australian timbers and our early craftsmen that had launched us onto the path of specializing in this field.

When we visited the multi-millionaire's home we fell in love with the secretaires. They were indeed stunning, especially seen as a pair, side by side in the man's wide marble tiled foyer. Annabelle had brought her camera, and with the new owner's permission took photo after photo. She used her magnifying glass to look at the inlays and the stringing. When the man led me off to a room to show me some of his other recent purchases, she stayed behind, and when we returned we found her lying on the floor trying to get a shot of the maker's initials at the base. The collector was somewhat bemused by her passion; he said she must come back whenever she wanted to look at them.

***

One week after our visit that house was robbed, *and one of the secretaires was taken*. The collector had a separate storage room at the side of the house and he had moved one of the twins into there while he was having some of the tiles in the foyer repaired. The thieves stole only from this room, but they completely stripped it.

We went to see the man again. He was very upset at the loss – and particularly because the pair *had now been split*. I spoke to his curator, a man I knew quite well – we had sometimes competed at auctions – and he said that they had alerted the whole antiques world and were fairly confident they would get it back. "It's too well known – they won't be able to do anything with it."

The collector decided that he would not make the remaining piece available to the National on its own; he would wait until the pair was re-united.

***

I formed the opinion that the thieves would not have known the special value of this secretaire – that they had simply filled up their van. However, with the ensuing publicity, they would certainly have realised what they had taken, and that it was too hot to try to pass on. What would they do? I thought they might well just dump it somewhere, hopefully tipping off the owner as to its whereabouts.

When the Carhew had not turned up within a month I thought that the thieves might now have decided to try and make some money from it after all, but to do that they would certainly need to *change its appearance*. Annabelle agreed, and she turned her mind to what that could involve.

First, she said, they would have to remove the pediment; it was too distinctive, and the piece would still look alright without one – or they could put a simpler one in its place. The kangaroo handles too would have to go – the more anonymous round "mushroom" ones found on Victorian pieces would do as replacements.

The inlays depicting the gum leaves would be more of a challenge. The thieves *could* just paint over the whole piece, but that would render it unattractive to most antique buyers. And there would be the risk – the real risk – that a buyer might strip off the paint, and then the jig would be up. A better idea she thought would be for them to *stain it,* and *very dark;* some cedar pieces at that time *were* being presented in a very dark stain, almost a purple, so that wouldn't seem too unusual. The inlay detail would then "disappear".

The diamond patterned astragal feature of the bookcase doors could be replaced by plain glass; finally, it would be quite easy to cut off those distinctively Georgian feet and replace them with later turned ones – what we call "bun" feet.

When all those things had been done, one would have, as she said, not a *Georgian* secretaire but a *Victorian* one: not a particularly attractive one, at first glance, but saleable.

I rang the collector's curator – he had heard nothing. I put to him our theory of alteration and he agreed that it was plausible. I told him my wife and I were keen to track down the missing piece and asked him to give me the measurements of the surviving piece, specifically the body, minus pediment and feet.

***

Annabelle and I set off then, in 1966, in pursuit of the Carhew. I thought we had as much chance of coming upon it as anyone; we were very active in the antiques trade – we were beginning to specialize in early Australian furniture – and we had a wealth of contacts.

We did not expect it to turn up at high-end auctions, nor to be presented in any of our top shops. If it were to appear anywhere, we reasoned, it would be at a more down-market venue – but that of course still left an awful lot of possibilities.

We let shop owners and dealers know that we were in the market for a cedar Victorian secretaire, not necessarily in good condition, but of a specific size. We knew the men who conducted the more 'everyday' auctions, and asked them to let us know if something of that order came up.

***

Well, we did receive a lot of phone calls from dealers and auctioneers over the years that followed – the *many* years – but with no result. I couldn't guess how many kilometres we travelled – but at least we only went to look at ones whose measurements were correct, or close; that still meant however looking at a lot of secretaires. I actually bought quite a few too, if they were good, and good value; we were dealers after all.

***

I realised early on that if our theory on renovation was correct, then somewhere there could be a loose set of carved cedar kangaroo handles. I began to advertise, in the regular antiques magazine that nearly all dealers get, for any old and interesting wooden drawer and door handles, preferably carved.

It is quite wonderful the number and variety of handles that are out there and, once again, I *bought*. Eventually I filled several shelves in the shed behind our shop in Camberwell, and there were always restorers in there rifling through them. I became not only 'the secretaires man' but 'the handles man' as well.

No luck with kangaroo handles however for five years – advertising in every issue of the magazine – then, a call from Kyneton. They sounded right; I could not leave the business that day because an important buyer was coming so Annabelle took the car. She rang back from the man's house to say that she had them!

The seller had picked them up at a church jumble sale four years before, but he knew nothing about any secretaire – the tree from which these fruit had fallen.

At least though we now had confirmation that some renovation had taken place. But, my friend, *that was it* – no sight or even hint of the missing Carhew *for another twenty years.*

In that time we continued to run our business – very successfully – building up our reputation as a source of good early Australian pieces, being busy, busy – but never giving up the search. Wherever we went, whatever we did, we were always – *always* – on the alert for it. But never a trace.

Annabelle was if anything even more determined than I was. I greatly admired the piece of course but I think I had a *male* attitude to the search – that old hunting instinct perhaps ? But with Annabelle it was different – it was almost as if she was trying to find *a member of the family* – a missing child. The Carhew Twin might have been one of *our* twins.

It was on the Australia Day weekend of 1991 that our feet were placed on the path that eventually led us to your town here on the Murray. Annabelle and I had taken off on a short tour of the near west of the state and on the Monday were in Daylesford.

We went to a café in the main street for lunch, and instead of walking straight back to the car, we detoured through a couple of the back streets – we like the old stone buildings in that town. We came to a big barn of a place with stuff spilling out onto the pavement: "Crabb's Treasures".

On the pavement were typical rural "collectables" – old scythes and buckets, gold sieves, wooden benches etc. – but I glanced inside as we drew level with the entrance and I could see some old furniture. We went in, and strolled along the aisles, between cupboards and wardrobes and chiffoniers – all bone dry and dusty and in need of much T.L.C. – that kind of shop – and actually the kind of shop we loved, and in which we had over the years found some of the treasures that will be in this auction.

We got chatting with the proprietor and soon realised that he knew his stuff. We talked trade for a while and Annabelle asked about secretaires; Crabb said, as I would have expected, that he saw them only rarely.

I told him that we were interested in a very early Victorian one or a Georgian one if possible and he said we would have liked the one he had had *about five years before*. He said it was Victorian but it had good cock-beading around the drawers. It had been "fiddled with" a bit – for one thing the glass in the doors had been replaced.

Then he said something that literally brought up the hairs on my neck. He said the drawers had the usual round handles but he could see they were replacement for what, by the old screw holes, were obviously long rectangular ones.

I glanced across at Annabelle and saw that her antennae were up too. She asked if the piece were plain or decorated in any way and he said it was quite plain but had been stained – "badly – too dark really, for cedar" – but then he said he thought he could make out some stringing under the stain. By now *we* were strung.

Crabb told us there had been a death – an old woman with no family – and her executor had dropped in lots of her old pieces to sell on consignment.

I said – as calmly as I could; I was in danger of babbling – that this was just the sort of piece we were looking for – did he remember who bought it? Perhaps we could go and see them and they might let us buy it. He said that it had been bought by a couple "from up on the Murray" – they had been having a short holiday in the area. He would have a record of their names.

He led us to his office, a booth absolutely crammed with boxes of papers, some of which were spilling out onto the floor. How would he find *anything*?

He must have read my mind because he said "don't worry, I know just where to look", and in fact did go straight to a particular box and begin to rifle through it. I was so keyed up that I was almost wetting myself – if I may express myself so indelicately.

After a few minutes of sorting and muttering however, Crabb said that, of all his records, he couldn't find this one. But not to worry, because the transport company he used was only about three blocks away, and they would have *their* records.

I wasn't at all confident that that would be the case, and spent our night at a local motel tossing and turning.

The next morning we were in that office first thing. It was a little family company and the wife did the bookwork. She said she did not keep records that far back. Did she remember the item? She shook her head. Would the driver remember anything? She said it would have been her father-in-law, and he had since passed away.

Greatly disappointed, we walked out of her office but she called us back. She said that if Crabb had said it was going up onto the Murray then it would normally have gone to the depot of another small company up there and she could tell us *their* name and address. Wilkinson's – *our Wilkinson's here.*

We went back to Melbourne and I rang Wilkinson's first thing the next morning. I had trouble getting the office girl to grasp what I was trying to find out. She said somewhat exasperatedly that she was the only person there, the men all being out, and that in any case it could take quite a while to find what I was looking for. I eased out of the conversation because I had already decided that I would go up immediately.

I made it to Wilkinson's yard by one o'clock. It was Cheryl Ridge in the office – she was Cheryl Simpson then. She called Reg Wilkinson over from the shed at the back; that's the father of the present Reg.

He did not need to look up any records. He remembered the piece; he had taken it straight out to the Johannson's – you know where their farm is – about twenty k's out on South Road.

I didn't wait to ring but drove straight there – only to find that *they no longer had it!* Lucy Johannson said it had been her mother-in-law who had bought it in Daylesford. After the older woman died, three years before, Lucy and her husband had moved from the cottage into the homestead and she decided she wanted to re-furnish the house. Her father-in-law had agreed that they could sell all the old things..

Wally Flatman used to run clearing sales then whenever clients sold their farms – well, the same as he does now. He told the Johannsons that he had one coming up in a month, and at a farm just down the road from them; he suggested that they enter their things in that as 'invited vendors".

Lucy Johannson said that there was a good turn-up on the day – as there usually is at these things, in my experience – and everything sold. She had no idea who bought the secretaire – she referred to it as a' bookcase'. Greg Johannson, who had by now come in from his outside work, couldn't remember either.

More disappointment – but at least we were closer; the Daylesford piece would probably still be in the district.

***

I went to see Flatman straight away. Yes, he did recall the sale, but no, he did not remember who had bought the secretaire, did not in fact remember it or any of the pieces. Would he still have the sale records? No, it was just a little clearing sale, with only the locals there; he said he'd probably just scribbled down the winning bidders initials or names on bits of paper and then destroyed them after settlement.

I described the piece in more detail but it was no use; it was pretty obvious that one piece of old furniture was much the same as another to that man. I asked if he could remember if there were any strangers at the sale – I was thinking that antique dealers from the region might well have turned up – but he said that no, they had all been locals.

I rang Annabelle about all this and she was very excited. She urged me to go back to the agent; if he said they had all been locals then he would be able to tell me *who they were*.

The next morning I was in his office early. He asked me more about myself this time, and why I was looking for this piece; I had decided on my 'story'. I had already told him that I was an antiques dealer in Melbourne and now I said that a client had commissioned me to find their old family piece, which had great sentimental value.

When I asked him to give me the names of the people who had been at the sale, so that I could contact them, he looked cautious about it; was he thinking I wondered that I might be some con artist from the big smoke trying to work some scam on simple country folk? I suggested that if he made a list of the people who were there, or who he thought *might* have been there, he could phone them first. Could we perhaps start to make the calls from this office, and now, if he had the time?

He must not have had too much on his plate that morning because he set to work. Within a few minutes he had a list of twenty names, and began ringing. The third call was answered and after he explained my mission he handed over the phone to me. It was Myrna Frick; yes, she remembered the sale and yes, she and her husband had bought some of the furniture but nothing big like the secretaire.

Could she remember the secretaire? Yes. Could she remember who bought it? No. Could she remember who else was there? She listed several of the names Flatman had given me plus a couple of others. During my call Flatman also had remembered two more.

He dialled several more numbers, explaining to me that most of the people were farmers and he did not expect we would get them during the day. Flo Gibbs did answer; no joy again, but from her one extra name.

The agent had listened openly to my phone conversations and was obviously now reassured about me. He said why didn't I continue to make the calls myself, and invited me to make them from his office. We went to the Royal later for lunch; by that time I had already reached eight people.

I was somewhat cheered; I had started with a list of twenty-five people and was now down to seventeen; surely amongst the remainder there would be the person who had bought the secretaire. I would work my way through the remainder of numbers from home in Melbourne, calling in the evenings.

Over the next week I did reach all those people *but with no result*. I got an extra two names in the process but no joy there either. Yet all said they could remember no stranger there, no "foreigner" – the consensus was that it had been "just the usual mob".

Mystery: *no-one* had bought the secretaire – but Flatman had said he was sure that *everything had sold*.

***

Annabelle and I were now at sixes and sevens. We continued with our business of course, but our hearts and minds were elsewhere – up here on the Murray River. Our obsessive desire had grown even stronger. Like a plant that had been neglected for years and was now receiving water and care, it was flourishing. I for one found I could think of nothing else.

I began to entertain the idea of leaving our shop in Melbourne in the sole care of Annabelle and taking up residence in this town for a time, so that I could follow up our leads, or chase new ones – on foot as it were. I had convinced myself that the Daylesford secretaire

– which might or might not have been the Carhew (but this was by far the best lead we had ever had) – was sitting in a house in this town or on a farm somewhere in the district. Remember, I am writing about the oldest known, quality piece of Australian made furniture – its twin in Melbourne – and the pair of immense value. Priceless. I *had* to track it down.

I put the idea of my relocating for a while to Annabelle, to find that *she* had been wrestling with the same idea; should *she* come here? We discussed it every day; in the end we decided it was probably better if *I* went. I would rent a house in the town for six months; I promised I would come back to her and the family often, possibly even every weekend.

***

Once settled in my new home I made a drawing of how we thought "our" secretaire now looked and rang all my local contacts again and asked to see them in turn. I showed the drawing to them, hoping it might jog some memories.

Two of the men and three of the women did remember it, but none could remember who had bought it. One said she had an impression it had *not* sold. After one month I was no nearer our goal.

I thought next of putting an advertisement in the local paper. This place was not big enough to support its own rag – and still isn't – but the paper published in Shepparton covered this area – as it does today.

At first I thought of "Public Notices" – asking anyone who had been present at the sale to phone me – but I decided that as I had already interviewed twenty six people who *had* been there, plus the auctioneer, and none of them could remember any other people, I thought I had covered that. So I decided to use the "Wanted" section; "looking for an old cedar secretaire. A good price will be paid."

I received just one reply, from a dealer in Echuca; he wanted to flog me a mahogany one.

***

I kept advertising, each month, but I also started to go to every clearing sale that I read or heard of, and within a radius of a hundred kilometres. And of course I called in at every antique and second-hand dealer's that I came across in my travels.

Most of the clearing sales were held mid-week but quite a few were held on weekends as well, so my visits back to Melbourne were not as frequent as I had promised Annabelle they would be. She was handling the business there perfectly well – and we talked every day on the phone – but the separation was a strain.

When however, towards the end of six months, I mentioned coming back to Melbourne she insisted we needed to keep looking here. "It's there darling, I know it is." She suggested that she come up and I go back and mind our shop.

***

We realised that in some respect the focus of our lives had shifted – to this place, and the tracking down of the Carhew. It became clear to us that we could not continue our search at this level and run our business in Melbourne.

Three things began to run through my mind. One, that if I were to continue to do my searches thoroughly I would need to begin door knocking, the houses in the town at first and then the surrounding farms as well. That was going to take a lot of time. Two, that I was getting to like this other home, with its position on the river, the friendliness of everyone, the pace of life. On the two occasions Annabelle had managed to come up she had liked it too. And three – and this took longest to form – that it would be quite possible to *run our business from here.*

I hesitated for a long time before putting this last idea to Annabelle. We had a very comfortable home – she had her friends and gym classes and her bridge club – and our daughters with their husbands and children lived close by. She would be giving up her life.

In fact though it was she who put the plan to me. "Darling, we've got to move. We've *got* to find this thing. It's too important; and this is the closest we have ever been. I know we love Melbourne and our life here but – we wouldn't be so very far away: three hour's drive. We can come down on weekends – every weekend if we like – or the girls can come up."

***

So we bought this shop and moved all the stock up from Melbourne. We put our Camberwell place on the market and got a good price for it, enough to buy a nice house here three times over. In fact the house we bought was the one I had been renting. And we found business did not slacken off at all, because, as I said, it was mostly initiated by phone calls anyhow. That antiques magazine even ran an article on our move, with photographs. And, within a week, Annabelle was playing bridge.

***

So we started on our beat, in the town first, house by house, block by block and street by street, sometimes Annabelle and sometimes me. We got no result – and it took us most of a year. Then we began tackling the farms; we drove up and down every road in this district – and for the next five years! (And as I write that, it hits me once again, the sheer *unlikeliness* of what we were doing. It *was* obsession – as we readily would have agreed).

But it never felt like a chore. You see, we "knew" we were close to our fabulous goal, and that in a way every negative result brought us closer. That's how we looked at it.

I had kept up the fiction here that we were looking on behalf of a wealthy Melbourne family and most of the farmers and farmer's wives knew about that, from the grapevine. They were curious, and welcoming when we called – lots of tea and cake – and we were usually asked to look at their own treasures. I even bought a few things; hardly any were good enough for our shop, but I wholesaled them off to other dealers in Melbourne.

***

Then – hallelujah! – Lucy Johannson, the woman whose parents-in-law had bought the secretaire in Daylesford, rang. "Come straight out!" she said. " It's here in our neighbour's shed – where we had the auction sale."

Imagine my feelings as I drove those twenty kilometres! You probably *can't* imagine them – no-one could. The search was over – at least for the Daylesford piece – and, could it be – *could it be* – that the thing Annabelle and I had searched for, not just these last years here but for *thirty* years – was just down this road in a farm shed?

***

I pulled in behind Lucy's neighbour's house. Lucy hurried out of the big shed and practically dragged me inside. "I rang Bill Foster to borrow a pitchfork and he said just look on the back wall. And there it is" she said, and pointed to a row of things against the back wall. Towards one end was a secretaire – grey with dust and with poultry droppings all down the front. "It hadn't been sold at all .The only thing that *hadn't* sold. We didn't realise that – and Wally Flatman's staff just left it in the shed at the end of the day. They must have all forgotten about it, and Bill Foster just left it there too."

I stared – *there it was – it* – and I mean the *big* it. Even from the entrance to the shed I could make out the faint outline of the gumleaf stringing under the dark stain, and then as I got closer I

214

could see the faint marks where the screws for the kangaroo handles had been. *I had found it!*

Apart from being very dusty and dry, it was exactly as Annabelle and I had thought it would be – no pediment, plain glass, and standing on thick bun feet – an ordinary looking, uncared for Victorian secretaire.

I went to it, as reverently as if I were approaching a shrine. I lowered the top drawer, to look at the desk. Surprisingly it was almost pristine inside, with all the pigeonholes and little drawers intact; at least Foster had not let his chooks nest in it. I opened one of the doors of the upper bookcase and could see that all the shelves were there.

"So you still own it Lucy?"

"Well – technically yes, I suppose so." As she was saying this a Landcruiser pulled up and the owner of the property walked into the shed. Lucy introduced me to Bill Foster and told him her story of the secretaire.

"Well it's still your's Lucy, if you want it," he said.

I turned to Lucy; my heart was pounding.

"Will you sell it to me?"

"Sell it! It's your's! After all your work? Take it. You've earned it."

I drove into town and got my van and was back at the shed in half an hour. But can you imagine the thoughts that were going through my head in that time? I had found – or Lucy had led me to – the most valuable piece of Australian furniture in existence. I knew it belonged to the man who had been robbed – and by now his family – and Lucy Johannson, thinking it belonged to *her* family, was giving it to *me!*

I knew the correct thing to do was to tell the woman exactly what this object was and to propose that she – or both of us – contact the collector's family or their employee the curator straight away. But *could* I do the correct thing? I had spent so much of my life – *too much* – in search for it. By the time I arrived back at the shed the Devil had done his work.

And at this point are you feeling uneasy old friend? Are you thinking that perhaps I am about to tell you I acted dishonourably – that you are going to learn something about me that you really will not want know? I am afraid so.

I imagine you have sometimes thought of me as a driver of hard bargains? Perhaps also someone who can at times play things close to his chest – not an *open* person? But – I hope – a man of his word? Even honourable? Well, not in this one matter I am afraid.

***

Lucy had waited at the shed. She had rung her husband and told him about the find. He had readily agreed that I should have the secretaire. I thanked her again and she helped me put it into the van; as you know, cedar is very light, and it was easily managed.

As I drove back to town I thought I was probably the happiest and most excited man in Australia – possibly the whole world – and no, sad to say, awareness of my perfidy did nothing at all to dampen my joy.

The next morning I dropped in at Flatman's to tell him about the find, but Lucy had already rung him. He was flabbergasted that he had made the mistake of believing that everything at that clearing sale had sold. "If I'd remembered that it hadn't sold, what a lot of work that would have saved you!" Yes, six years – but I was too euphoric to dwell on that.

He said he wanted to come and see it and we walked back up the street to my shed. He stood in front of it but did not really *see*; he had no idea just what he was looking at! He asked me if I had told the family in Melbourne and I said yes.

"They'll be happy."

"Ecstatic."

It was I who was ecstatic. In my little shed at the rear of my shop in this little town on the banks of the Murray River was *the* priceless piece of Australian heritage that Annabelle and I had pursued for so long. *And I simply could not countenance the thought of letting it go.* Yes, one day, I told myself, but not yet – not *now*. I wanted to keep it a while, to look at it – to look at every detail – to touch it – to marvel at what we had.

I was now sixty eight. What would it matter, I said to myself, if we kept it for a year – even for a few years – or perhaps even until I died? When it did join its mate, it would still be a great event; in fact, the longer it was missing the more sensational would be its return. How much more of a drawcard would it be for the National Gallery then when both pieces came to together. And – in the meantime – would we really be hurting anyone? That is how I rationalised.

***

When I told Annabelle that I wanted to keep it for a while before returning it to its rightful owners she said that I shouldn't, but did not say much more. As the weeks went by – turning into months – she would say something now and then, but she never harangued me.

I cleaned it and we put it in our lounge room – an everyday Victorian secretaire, if anyone ever looked at it.

Months turned to years; every now and then Annabelle would make the case for returning it. I would say 'just a little bit longer' and she would drop it. I don't think our secret worried her a lot – and I knew she would never tell anyone about our "guest".

***

When the awful cancer took her, and so suddenly, I did think that that was the time to turn the secretaire in – but I found then that the piece meant even more to me. My rock had gone – but this was the replacement – my *one good thing*. The secretaire and Annabelle and I had shared a thirty year history and I wanted the two of us remaining to stay together.

***

Anyhow – it is still here. I know you will be agog to see it – and it is in fact right in front of you – *inside* this reproduction secretaire; I had it made supersize so I could hide it there.

I asked you if you could notice anything unusual about this piece. Have you spotted it? If not – *it is joined on the mid-line* – from the pediment to the base, but the join all but invisible. Can you see it now?

Observe how shallow the desk is, compared to the depth of the whole piece. Pull out one of the drawers and you will see that it too is very short. Likewise the shelves in the bookcase are very narrow; this big reproduction secretaire is *occupied*.

Do you know those little Victorian writing boxes that open to become miniature desks? Some have secret drawers, which can only be opened by activating a hidden catch. This secretaire has one of those.

Pull out the third from the top of the right hand drawers. Pull it right out and put your hand in. Feel a raised rounded metal button? Press it firmly; you should hear a low clunk. You have just undone a latch behind those pigeon-holes. Now put one hand on each side of the front of the secretaire and push. The two halves will swing open – and reveal the obsession of my life.

***

Have you recovered yet? Ready to phone Allingham the curator ? His phone number and address are on the extra piece of paper in this envelope. Give him this letter so that he has the whole story.

The existence of this letter will make the handing over of the secretaire even more newsworthy – will even increase its value. It adds to its story – it is great *provenance* as we say; if the people who stole it thirty years ago would only come forward and tell *their* story the curator would have it all.

His job now will be to bring the piece back to the way it was before its "renovation". By the way the kangaroo handles are in its top left hand drawer.

Whoever works on the restoration will need to get some of that old thin glass for the bookcase doors, and recreate the astragal and cut the glass to fit. And make a new pelmet and replace the feet. They will then have to bring the old polish to life again too, but really that won't be hard. That curator might want to let the Gallery do it; they have some wonderfully experienced restorers – and they will have its twin to use as their guide. Piece of cake; they will make it look exactly like that twin.

***

But what, I wonder, are you thinking about your old friend? A crook? Silly old coot? I had thought that the catalogue you are compiling would be my legacy, but I am wondering now if that is so. Will it be this fantastic piece of our heritage – and will people remember me because I was so diligent in tracking it down, with such determination and over such a long time, *or* because I then hoarded it? It's theft isn't it, to keep something that does not belong to you? But I was only holding it for a while; it was always going back.

Thank you once again old friend, and goodbye.

THE WRITER

Ron Iddon is probably best known in Australia for his work on the ABC's long running television series "A BIG COUNTRY", as reporter and director.

He left the ABC to become an independent filmmaker, eventually writing and directing twenty more documentaries, all of which were shown on television; "Peppimenarti", about life in an Aboriginal settlement in the Northern Territory, was nominated for 'Best Documentary' in the AFI Awards.

He has three (co-written) non-fiction books to his credit, "A Big Country 1 and 2" and "The Stockman". This is his first published work of fiction.

Ron lives in Toowoomba, southern Queensland. He writes every day, and is also a part-time teacher of literacy; his recreation is the study and sometimes restoration of antique furniture.

★ *"The Morning News" and "The Waitress", both included in this book, have won awards for the writer.*